NIGHTHAWK!

TO SEAN —
MAY YOU FIND
YOUR OWN
FLYWAYS!

NIGHTHAWK!

Jamie Bastedo

Red Deer Press

Published in Canada by Red Deer Press, 195 Allstate Parkway, Markham, ON L3R 4T8
www.reddeerpress.com

Published in the United States by Red Deer Press, 311 Washington Street, Brighton, Massachusetts 02135

Edited for the Press by Peter Carver
Cover and interior design by Daniel Choi

We acknowledge with thanks the Canada Council for the Arts, and the Ontario Arts Council for their support of our publishing program. We acknowledge the financial support of the Government of Canada through the Canada Book Fund (CBF) for our publishing activities.

 ONTARIO ARTS COUNCIL
CONSEIL DES ARTS DE L'ONTARIO **Canada Council** **Conseil des Arts**
for the Arts **du Canada**

Library and Archives Canada Cataloguing in Publication
Bastedo, Jamie, 1955-
    Nighthawk! / Jamie Bastedo.
ISBN 978-0-88995-455-7
    I. Title.
PS8553.A82418N54 2012   jC813'.6   C2012-905182-9

Publisher Cataloging-in-Publication Data (U.S.)
Bastedo, Jamie.
    Nighthawk! / Jamie Bastedo.
[256] p. : cm.
Summary: The spirited and inspiring adventures of Wisp, a nighthawk who migrates from the tropical rainforests of Columbia to the northern Tundra, in an effort to get farther north than any of his species has ever been before.
ISBN: 978088995-4557 (paper)
1. Hawks – Juvenile fiction. I. Title.
[Fic] dc23   PZ7.3484Ni 2012

Manufactured by Friesens Corporation in Altona, MB, Canada, in October 2012
Job # 77531

MIX
Paper from
responsible sources
FSC® C016245

To Jazzy, Riley, and the kids of Back Bay.

Prologue

*N*ear *the top of the world, in a school shaped a bit like a frog, at the back of a case of basketball trophies, hangs a gold-framed photo of three brown speckled birds. Two are perched side by side on the school's pebble roof. They look up, cringing, at a third bird, mostly blurred, as it swoops in for a wide-winged landing almost on top of them.*

No one remembers how that photo ended up with the trophies, but it seems to fit. Someone is obviously proud of it.

You could easily walk by that photo and see no birds at all. That's the way it is with nighthawks. They are mysterious birds, hard to see, hard to find, hard to figure out.

If you see one on the ground, you might mistake it for a rock or a stick or a crusty piece of lichen. If you see one in the air, you might mistake it for a wobbling bat or a high-flying hawk or a dagger-winged falcon. If you see the bright flash of a nighthawk's wingbars, as it dips and dives through the dusk, you might even mistake it for a UFO.

But you could never mistake the sound it makes when it plunges out of nowhere and sets the whole sky shaking. Like the blurred bird in the photo, nighthawks are too fast to capture, too mysterious to know.

Except, that is, if you're lucky enough to journey with one into its magical, dangerous world.

1

Death from Above
Moosehead School, Yellowknife, Northwest Territories

I know I have a problem when the stars return. Even the planets give me grief.

I can't read them.

That's what we Plebeians do.

That's why Guardians let us live.

Where Damon gazes up at the stars, with that odd look in his eyes, and sees a pouncing jaguar or hovering rhinoceros beetle, I see random blips of light. Where he sees a flock of nighthawks diving at Saturn or a giant raven dive-bombing the North Pole, I see a mess of bright squiggles and dots.

I can see stars clear enough. I just can't read them like he does. Like he badly wants me to.

Damon, my father, is a fully initiated Navigator.

In the star department, I'm a nothing.

Things go okay until I discover that.

I remember feeling totally at home, peeking out from under my mother's breast, her soft brood feathers tickling my beak. At three weeks old, I'm almost ready for my first test flight from the flat pebble roof of Yellowknife's Moosehead Public School. But my feathers are too stubbly, so I spend most of the day tucked beneath Fern, my mother, without a care in the world.

Except for Winnie and Willo, my brother and sister. Luckily, they always sleep in and I can enjoy the best time of day without any pokes or bumps or full-blown attacks.

What wakes me is Mom's habit of turning to the sunrise. She purrs and coos as she settles back down on us while I stare at the sky. I'm totally fine with doing that since, in mid-July, the sky is still too bright at night for any stars. They aren't a problem for me. I don't know yet how much they will hurt me.

I like to guess the spot where the sun will crack the horizon. I like to listen to the dawn breeze as it gets the poplar tree swaying beside the school. Its branches reach over the roof and swish in front of me. What I like most about this time of day are Dad's air shows.

Beerb ... Beerb ... Beerb.

I stick my beak into the world and tilt my head to the sky.

There he is, circling high above the school. Set on fire by the rising sun, Dad's wings slice the air with a whistle and a whoosh that raise the feathers on my back. I struggle to follow his dizzying flight as he darts like a swallow, hovers like a tern, soars like a hawk.

Beerb ... Beerb ... Beerb.

Then silence ...

My lungs freeze. My spine tingles. Time stops.

Dad pulls in his wings and drops into a tailspin, spiraling straight for us. Just when I'm sure he'll crash, he fans his wings, spreads his tail feathers, and makes a sound that gets my whole body shivering with delight.

V-R-R-R-O-O-O-O-M!

Dad ends his show with a cool inside loop, lands on the branch closest to us, and perches crosswise on it.

For some reason, this always bugs Mom. Not the show. He basically does that for her. And to tell other nighthawks, *Get lost, this roof is ours!* It's the way he sits. Nighthawks are supposed to perch *lengthwise* on a branch, not across it. But that's my dad.

By this time, my siblings are awake and the fights begin, for space, for attention, for food. Especially food.

Mom goes hunting for us while Dad watches for ravens. "Good morning, chicklets," Mom says when she comes back, through a mouthful of crunched-up dragonflies.

Winnie is the biggest chick, so guess who gets fed first? He shoves Willo and me out of the way, then pecks like crazy at Mom's beak. I could easily push Willo aside, over the edge if I wanted. But I don't. I let her eat next.

When it's my turn, I open my big mouth, Mom shoves her beak halfway down my throat, and out comes breakfast. I usually get more than anyone else since I've learned to clamp onto Mom's feet and not let go until she has nothing more to give.

"Fast learner," Dad says.

It's the same routine day after day.

Until Winnie gets picked off.

It happens one stinking hot afternoon. Dad says the

summers are getting hotter and this is the hottest day yet. We've grown lots, but Mom insists we stay crammed under her, out of the blazing sun. The heat turns the tar under the pebbles into black, oozing muck.

Dad hasn't budged from his poplar perch since the sun came up. He stays locked in some kind of trance, with one eye closed, the other cocked to the sky.

"Let's fly to the lake and catch dragonflies!" Winnie says.

Sounds good to me. I can't wait to fly.

Mom raises her wings to blow off some heat. "With those baby feathers, you'd be over the edge and under a car before you could say *road kill.*"

"I'll teach you some tricks," Dad says, snapping out of his trance.

"Oh no, you won't," Mom says. "Let them master the basics first."

"What kind of tricks, Dad?" I ask.

"Oh, well there's—"

"I want to catch dragonflies, too!" Willo whines. "You never let us go anywhere." She pops out from under Mom and hops, head down, straight for the roof edge.

"*Chuck-chuck!*" Fern snaps. "Willo, get back here!" She cuts off Willo and shoves her into the shade of the poplar branch.

I'm about to bolt for the edge when Winnie beats me to it.

"Ow-ow-ow-ow-ow-ow!" He's waded into a patch of scorching tar. "Get me out of this yucky stuff! *Owww!*"

Both Mom and Dad zoom over to help.

Mom head-butts Winnie backwards.

"Go! Go!" Dad yells at Mom. "Keep the others out of this stuff!"

"Winnie, you goof!" I yell, hopping closer. "Why don't you watch where you're—"

Mom slams me against the poplar branch.

Dad sweeps his wings under Winnie's belly and fights to pull him out. Winnie's new feathers, just a few days from being flight-ready, are coated with hot tar.

"Ow-ow-ow-ow!"

"Stop squirming!" Dad shouts. "Just let me—"

I freeze to the slow *whuhh-whuhh-whuhh-whuhh-whuhh* of big wide wings. Through a trembling screen of poplar leaves, I catch the gleam of spread-out raven feathers.

Dad leaps into the air, shrieking, "*Dick-a-dick-a-dick-dick-dick-dick-dick,*" at the raven. He lunges at it again and again.

The raven ignores him, swoops down on my big brother, and plucks him off the roof.

The awful silence that follows is torn open by Mom's scream. "Winnie! *Winnie!*"

2

Navigator

Moosehead School, Yellowknife, Northwest Territories

With Winnie dead, that makes me the oldest son, Dad's apprentice Navigator. My lessons start the very next day.

Seems harsh maybe, but the days are getting shorter and there's a restlessness in the air. The territories of other birds are starting to break up and the flocking already has begun. The stars still have not shown themselves so Dad has to arrange pebbles on the roof to teach me their names.

It seems so easy at first.

Dad chooses a shady spot beside the poplar branch where the pebbles are thin and the cooler tar is jet black— like the night sky I have yet to see. He starts by clearing a big circle of tar with his wingtip, then adds one pebble at a time.

"These are the primary navigational stars," he says and calls out each by name.

The Boreal star, the Quill star, Scapular, Hallux, Tarsus, Barbule.

He asks me to repeat each star's name over and over. He makes a game of it by having me look away while he removes one star or shifts it around. When I look back, I have to tell him what's different. This hurts my head but we usually end up laughing.

So far, so good.

"Time to learn your constellations," Dad says at the start of my next lesson. He sweeps a bunch more pebbles into the circle. He carefully shapes them into animals and birds, beetles and butterflies, mountains and rivers.

I struggle to keep everything in my head. I really work hard to see what he sees.

Mostly I don't.

"You have to use your imagination at first," he says. "It'll come."

By shifting just a few pebbles, he conjures up entire landscapes, each with their own stories. A jungle full of monkeys and snakes. A bald desert flecked with cacti and canyons. And my favorite, the one that brings a special glimmer to Dad's eyes, a vast treeless land where the sun never sets, teeming with caribou, brimming with bugs.

The Tundra. *Where I'm going. Even if it's forbidden.*

I totally get the stories. I eat them up and feel it's in my blood to learn them. What I don't get are all the shapes and patterns Dad keeps throwing at me.

I can't see them. They're just random pebbles.

Dad often looks up from his pebble pictures, saying, "Do

you understand this?" or "Do you see it, Wisp?" and I always nod yes, even if I don't. He can usually tell if I'm faking it and goes over everything one more time.

But it's no use.

I know I'm really lost when Dad starts showing me which direction the constellations move, where they rise, where they set, how each planet cuts a path through them at different times of year ...

Stop!

But he doesn't stop. The next day he moves on to the most important lesson of all.

Flyways.

Dad shows me how the constellations are joined to each other through a web of flyways that nighthawks have used forever. "Navigators like us must learn all the flyways," he says.

Hmm. Navigators like us.

"That's the only way we can guide other nighthawks up and down the continents during migration," he says.

My head's about to spin off.

Dad senses this. "You're a fast learner, Wisp. You can do this." He looks over at Mom and Willo, asleep in the sun. "You have to. For them. For our Colony."

No pressure, eh, Dad?

I stare at the pebbles. That's all they are. Pebbles. My only hope is that all this navigation stuff gets easier when the real stars come out.

It only gets worse.

The stars come out the same day the fire hits.

It's mid-August, another sweltering day when the tar is bubbling hot. The wind is so strong it blows loose pebbles off the roof. Willo and I have been flying for only a few weeks, but already I've been toying with a few of Dad's stunts—which I'm way happier to learn than star maps. The incredible wind seems like a fun way to test my budding aerobatic skills. But Mom will have none of it and grounds Willo and me until things blow over.

The wind gets even wilder after the sun goes down, blood-red.

Willo is the first to smell the smoke. Soon we taste it in the air. Then it's gushing out of the forest straight for town. The smoke seems to hug the ground as it tears past, leaving the evening sky above us strangely clear.

That's when I notice Dad staring at the sky. I follow his gaze to a faint cluster of lights I've never seen before.

My first stars.

"Do you see it, Wisp," he says, like we're in the middle of another lesson. But this is no lesson. "The pouncing jaguar."

I squint at a mess of stars. Totally random, just like the pebbles. *What jaguar?* My stomach shrinks. "Uh ... yeah."

"Are you sure, Wisp?"

He usually knows when I'm faking it. "Where, Dad?"

He points a wingtip right where I'm looking. "There." He's not looking at the stars any more. He's staring at me.

"Well, I—"

"Might we continue this lesson later?" Mom shouts over the insane wind. "Look behind you!"

I turn and see balls of fire dancing over the forest at the edge of town.

"It's coming right for us!" Willo cries.

Saved by the fire.

The four of us perch on a corner of the school roof,

watching the fire march out of the forest and into Yellowknife. It starts with a huge explosion at the edge of town that shoots flames as high as the tallest office tower. Then all the lights go out. House after house bursts into flames as the wind blows tongues of fire deep into the city. My eyes start watering so bad I can hardly see.

"Let's get out of here!" Dad shouts when cars and buses start exploding a few streets away. "Follow me!" He arches his wings for takeoff, then quickly folds them. He's looking up at the sky again.

"Please, Damon," Mom says. "This is no time for—"

"No, not stars," he says. "Can you hear it?"

Above the explosions and sirens and screaming, I hear a snarly roar rushing toward us.

"Okay, listen up, everybody," Dad yells.

I don't like the shake in his voice.

"If we get split up, we'll rendezvous at the mouth of the Slave River on the south side of Great Slave Lake. There's a big delta there, *major* landmark. Even a Guardian couldn't miss it. Just follow the foolproof flyway that joins the two brightest constellations, the Jaguar and the Butterfly. Remember, Wisp?"

"Yeah, yeah." *I may remember them, but I sure as heck don't see them.*

"Willo, you know them?" he says.

"Sure, Dad. You showed me the pebbles. We won't get split up, though, will we?"

Dad never gets a chance to answer. The roar becomes too deafening. I look up just in time to blast out of the way before a sideways waterfall drops out of the sky and blows apart smack on top of the school.

When I look back, all I see flying through the wind-ripped smoke and flames is a retreating water bomber.

Not a nighthawk in sight.

3

ESCAPE

The Refugium, Ecuador rainforest

Eight months later, I'm looking up through a suffocating shroud of knotted vines to a tiny disk of sky. In my mind, I've flown a million times through that one and only window to the outside world.

The Refugium's heavily guarded Sky Portal.

What an idiot I was to come here, to pride myself at finding the Refugium in the middle of the Amazon rainforest, only to discover that it's nothing but a glorified birdcage ruled by a bunch of bullies.

What an airhead to think that the Colony was where I belonged. The joke is, I'd worked my feathers to the quills to find this place. Risked my life for it many times.

Not long after losing my family in the Yellowknife fire, it hit me like another water bomber load.

I was alone.

After a couple of days, screaming my lungs out for my parents—embarrassing to think back now—I realized I had a choice. Suck it up or die.

So I sucked it up. Became my own best company. Well, safest company, anyway. But I was never really alone. To survive, I had to break one of our Colony's strictest rules. I made friends with other kinds of birds.

Trouble is, just weeks out of the nest, how was I supposed to know who was friend or foe? I learned fast that birds like chickadees, warblers, and thrushes were harmless enough. But they had little to teach me. What about thrashers and shrikes and cuckoos? What about ducks and geese and cranes? What could I learn from them? Through trial and error, and almost getting eaten more than once, I learned who I could trust. They became my teachers. I picked up life-saving skills, like how to find the best bugs, avoid predators, forecast weather, and dodge human stuff like wires and buildings.

Best of all, I learned some cool flying tricks. From terns to tanagers, my new friends couldn't teach me fast enough. You can blame Dad for that. He was an aerobatic fanatic.

But I learned nothing about navigation. It wasn't their fault. After the water bomber hit, and I couldn't find Dad's *foolproof* flyway to our emergency rendezvous on the Slave River—I just gave up. Totally. Traveling with other birds, I didn't pay attention to flyways, landmarks, wind currents, any of that stuff. As long as I could tag along with anyone basically headed south, I figured, why bust my skull trying to navigate? Let them do it.

I'm no good at it, anyway.

So what if I couldn't read stars? I could read birds. From them I learned what I had to do to survive. After that, it was all about aerobatics.

It was only when I'd crossed the Gulf of Mexico that I started missing my family again. Turned out that the golden plovers I'd been flying with were also aiming for the rainforest. I started asking birds we met about a big colony of nighthawks overwintering somewhere in Ecuador. Not much to go on, but that's all I knew.

From bird after bird, all I got was, "Never heard of it." Until I met an old toucan in Venezuela. He told me of seeing a huge flock of nighthawks and pointed the way with his fat red beak. "What a strange booming noise you birds make," he'd said. I left my plover friends and struck out alone across the Amazon rainforest, determined to find my family and winter home. I followed a dangerous trail of clues and tips that led to the very Sky Portal that now makes a joke of the freedom I once had.

The amazing family reunion I'd dreamed about during the last days of my journey fizzled as soon as I entered the Refugium. For one thing, no Dad. I was told he'd been roasted by the Yellowknife fire. Flattened by the water bomber. Wasted by starvation. Eaten by coyotes.

Exactly how my father died was anyone's guess.

I miss him like crazy but another thought dulls the pain. *At least my secret will be safer.* Dad won't be chipping it out of me every time he teaches me a new star story, trying to turn me into the Navigator I'll never be. I won't have to pretend I can read the stars.

It feels cruel to even think this but I can't help it.

And Mom, as shocked and happy as she was to see me

alive, soon started harassing me with Colony rules and commandments until I was ready to drown myself. I never let on how happy I was to see her. On the way down, I couldn't help thinking that water bomber might've wiped out my whole family.

Then there's Willo. She'd filled out a lot since I last saw her in Yellowknife. Her throat and breast feathers now show the buffy color of a more grown-up female. I hardly recognized her at first until she spoke in that high-pitched tone that can really bug me.

Now all I can dream about is getting out of here.

Before anyone discovers my secret.

It has almost leaked out lots of times. Like when I was on snake patrol around the edge of the Refugium with a group of juvenile Plebes like me. As usual, a couple of Guardians hovered above us, herding us along with their shouts and insults. The biggest one started questioning me about my trip south. Who did I travel with? What route did I take? How did I navigate? He was trying to collect dirt on me in case I acted up again.

I just answered him in one-word lies—Nobody. South. Stars.

When I mentioned stars, it was my fellow Plebes who started thumping me with questions, I guess knowing who my father was. That's when I started freaking inside. Luckily, somebody spotted a small tree viper. In the commotion of chasing it away, my supposedly brilliant knowledge of stars was forgotten before they tried to peck it out of me.

That was close.

Here I thought I'd come home a hero, that other juvenile

Plebes would admire me for what I'd done—flown solo all the way from the Boreal Forest. *Amazing!*

Instead, what I mostly got was envy, jealousy, even hatred. Calling me a liar, a fraud, a freak. Dissing my dad. That hurt more than anything.

Maybe it's because they were so bored in the Refugium. This place does something to your head, like everyone's on edge, wants to pick a fight. Maybe they're just taking out their frustrations on me instead of Guardians, which, of course, would be suicidal.

I later found out the name of that snoopy Guardian. Flare. A real power-trooper. He'll probably be Principal Guardian some day. He's got the fat feet and extra slashing claw like any other Guardian. The bigger beak with its razor edge. The gilded wingbars, not white like ours. But of the hundreds of nighthawks in our Colony, he's got to be one of the chunkiest. And has the worst breath. All skunky, like he's got a sweet beak for dead meat. I wouldn't put it past him.

But I don't have to worry about Flare any more. Or my secret getting out.

Now that I have an escape plan.

Nothing fancy. Just bust out when no one's looking. Through an unguarded portal.

I know they exist. I've heard other Plebes whisper about them. Heard the stories about birds mysteriously *disappearing through the cracks.* Heard Guardians grumble about *vagrant rebels*—sounds good to me—*who shun the comfort and security of the Refugium only to be ripped apart by jungle beasts.* How else could they have escaped, but through an unguarded portal?

The only trick was finding one.

Which I have. At least, if those monkeys weren't fooling with me. They're the ones who told me about it. But you never know with those guys.

I inspect the Refugium's fence of tangled creepers one more time. They drape over a stockade of giant trees with flared trunks that lock together in one thick wall. The Freedom Wall. That's what the Royals call it.

Yeah, tell me about freedom.

There's barely enough room in here for a decent loop-de-loop. Every time I try a flying stunt, some fat Guardian muscles me back to the ground. Threatens to throw me into the Hutch.

Like I say, a glorified birdcage.

"What are you doing, Wisp?"

I've been so absorbed in studying the ceiling that I don't hear Mom flutter down beside me. Like all other Plebes, she spends most of her days picking fire ants off the soggy jungle floor—that is, when she's not assigned to snake patrol. What else is there to do here? What else is there to eat? Not much.

Unless, of course, you're a Guardian or a Royal, winging free through the sunshine, gobbling down the juiciest rainforest bugs.

"Oh ... nothing."

Mom chokes down another beakful of fire ants. It pains me to watch her, to watch *any* self-respecting nighthawk do it. "When did you last catch a bug on the wing?"

Mom huffs. "Not this again. You know it's either ants or starve. Just look at you."

She's right. I've lost a lot of weight since arriving here

last fall. Not too smart if I'm planning to fly to the Tundra real soon. I should be pigging out. *But eating ants? Off the ground?* Humiliating.

I detect a muffled roar from the jungle. "Hear that?" I ask, grateful for a little diversion.

"What?"

"That roar."

"Just ignore it," Mom says.

"Jaguar." I'd love to see it bust in. Create a big fuss. Perfect distraction for me to bust out. "Has one ever made it through?"

"You know a jaguar could never pounce through the Freedom Wall."

"Freedom? Define freedom."

Mom snaps her beak at me. "There you go again, sounding just like your father."

"That's right," comes a polished voice above my head. "Willful. Unruly. Just like his father."

I look up at a female nighthawk whose feathers are frosted with age but perfectly trimmed. Her sleek body is parked lengthwise along a mossy branch in proper nighthawk style. Her branch, where only Royals may roost, droops from a gigantic two-story stump stuck in the eye of a black-water lagoon.

"Maybe you could help me then," I say in a neutral voice. "What is freedom, Arwen?"

"I beg your pardon."

Careful. I've pissed her off already.

"Sorry. What is freedom, *Your Greatness?*"

Arwen looks down at me with a fierce coolness that runs in her Royal blood.

"We are truly free here, juvenile. Free from *hunger*. In the Refugium, insects pour from every leaf and vine."

"Uh-huh," I say. "Fire ants for breakfast, lunch, and dinner."

"Silence, Plebeian," Arwen says in a whisper that raises my nape feathers. "May I remind you how we starved on the South Crossing, how your fellow nighthawks, too weak to fly, fell from the sky to be eaten by vultures and dogs."

"Uh … I wasn't there, remember?"

"Yes. And how fortunate that you have abandoned the reckless ways of a *vagrant*." She spits out that word like she'd swallowed acid.

Just wait, Your Haughtiness. Those days have just begun.

Arwen carries on in low rumbly tones. "In the Refugium, we are free from the whims of *weather*. Never too cold or hot. Never battered by storms or winds. Here the atmosphere is stable, predictable, safe."

And boring. Oh, to zoom through a nice bone-rattling thunderstorm. It won't be long now. I've found a way out and I'm feeling extra cocky. Maybe too cocky. "That's it then, a full belly and a cozy cage? *That's* freedom?"

Arwen opens her eyes wide. "Need I remind you, juvenile, that here in the Refugium, we also live free from *fear*. Free from jaguars, snakes, and vampire bats that will suck your blood dry. And, most of all, free from the dreaded Dark Ones that swoop out of the sky and snatch away nighthawks."

"Ravens? You know there aren't any—"

"The jungle skies are thick with predators that even ravens fear." Arwen's voice is rising.

My voice, too. "But the last raven I saw was, like, way back in Mexico. They never fly this far south. It's the law."

Arwen gives me a long, withering smile. "The law of the jungle is this: there *is* no law." Her words echo off the Freedom Wall for the whole Colony to hear. "The only laws we can trust are our own. The Three Noble Oaths. You, of course, know them by heart."

"Of course," I lie.

"Well, then?" Arwen says.

Mom nudges me with one wing. "Go on, Wisp, say the Oaths."

"I ... uh ... just *love* when you recite them, Your Greatness."

Arwen closes her eyes, raises her Royal beak, and harangues us, yet again, with her noble nonsense. "Blessed be our winter Refugium, for it saves us from all perils and hunger."

My insides flip at the thought of another *day* in this jungle jail.

Arwen opens her eyes a crack, waiting. I hold my breath. Then it comes, the mumbled monotone of Plebeian voices. Except mine. Maybe there are others. The required response comes later than ever. I take this as a sign of growing discontent.

Arwen does not seem fully satisfied but carries on to the Second Oath. "Blessed be the protection and guidance of Guardians during all our Crossings, North and South."

Make me puke. What protection did I need flying down here? And guidance? Let's get it right. Without Plebeian help, Guardians couldn't navigate their way out of a cornfield. Okay, maybe they can find a few landmarks. But like me, they can't read stars. That's basically why Guardians keep us alive. To safely steer them back and forth during migration.

Without Plebes, Guardians would probably go extinct. They know it. Hate it, too.

Again, there's a long pause before the masses respond to Arwen.

She grinds into the Third Oath. "Blessed be the Boreal Forest, our one true summer home, beyond which there can be no life or liberty."

There she goes again. Another swipe at the Tundra, pretending it doesn't exist. Like the world ends at the Boreal Forest. She just wants to keep us all pinned under her iron wing, even during the breeding season. *Well, I'll show her.*

This time the Plebeian response is weaker than ever. It's true, then. There are others like me. Those that keep silent, just moving their beaks. A punishable crime.

Maybe I imagine all this, but the very whiff of rebellion sparks something hot in me, curdling in my gizzard. I launch into the smothering air. I slam on the air brakes and hover in front of Arwen, forgetting that none but Royals can go anywhere near this branch. I have this mental block when it comes to rules. "You lock us in here for months and preach about freedom?"

"Silence, juvenile!" Arwen commands.

Uh-oh. Now I've done it.

Arwen points both wings at me, flashing her indigo wingbars, the telltale mark of all Royals. "Guardians, throw him in the Hutch!"

A faint wind rustles through the Refugium as hundreds of Plebes draw in their breath.

I lose all lift for a moment, then, finding my wings again, I pull away from Arwen to what I guess is a respectful distance. "Uh ... look, I'm sorry. I just need some air. Some light. I can't breathe in here."

"Arwen, please, no!" cries Mom who flutters up beside me. "He's already feeling cooped up. He couldn't—"

"Enough! I'll have no one flouting the laws of my Colony."

Two Guardians swoop down from the Freedom Wall and crowd in tight beside me. They jostle Mom out of the way and force me down to the lagoon. They drive my beak into the mud and a leech squirms into one nostril. I snort it out.

Both Guardians shove me across a slimy log that leads to a spooky crack at the base of the Royal stump.

The Hutch.

A lone Guardian voice starts up a chant. "Hutch! Hutch! Hutch! Hutch!"

Flare. Who else?

More voices ripple out from his and soon all Guardians join in from their command posts on the jungle floor, the Freedom Wall, the Sky Portal. "Hutch! Hutch! Hutch! *Hutch! Hutch!*"

Above their deafening chant, I hear a familiar screech from the ceiling. My Guardian captors look up, giving me enough slack to wriggle free.

I zoom past Arwen in time to see a thick purple blob land on her back.

"Bulls-eye!" screams a crazy voice from above.

I glimpse a bunch of mustached faces peeking through the ceiling vines. A gang of white-bellied spider monkeys vanishes into the leaves. I dart after them, bonking my head against a knot of jumbled vines. "Hey, wait!" I cry.

Maybe they were fooling with me. There is no portal.

I look down and see Arwen shoot from her perch, spraying purple goo on her subjects. A second volley of monkey crap spatters the two Guardians chasing me and they bank away from each other, shaking their wings in disgust.

"Don't let him escape!" Arwen cries.

Six more Guardians launch from hidden perches in the Freedom Wall.

I hover a feather-width below the green ceiling. *It's got to be here*, I think as I try to burn a way through with my eyes.

"Psst, psst. Over here!" hisses a spider monkey.

"Where?"

I hear the heavy flap of Guardian wings closing fast.

"This way!"

I spot a monkey's arm waving at me through a tiny gap in the vines. I lunge for it and scrabble in.

Above the wild pounding of my heart, I hear my sister's muffled cry. "Wisp! I'm coming with you!" I hesitate for an instant, just long enough for a set of Guardian claws to clamp down on my tail feathers. Flare's skunky breath fills the narrow portal. He's too bulky to fit in, but he easily pulls me backward over the slippery vines.

From the other end of the portal, a second set of claws grabs my belly, these ones attached to five leathery fingers. "Come on! You can do this!" shrieks a spider monkey. "Don't let go!"

4

ATTACK
Coco River, Ecuador rainforest

D *rat that Willo.* For a Plebe to just *think* about escaping is a crime—so what does she go and do? Scream about it with a dozen Guardians on her tail. Her words have rattled around in my head since the moment I shot through the unguarded portal into the sunshine.

Wisp! I'm coming with you!

When I glanced over my shoulder, I saw no sign of Willo or, thank the winds, any Guardians. Just a gang of spider monkeys waving up at me and smacking their hands together.

The question now clawing my mind: *What happened to Willo?* Got stuck in the portal? Nabbed by Flare? Thrown in the Hutch? Or worse?

Here I had the perfect escape plan and she had to wreck

it. How free am I really when all I can think about is my little sister? Especially when I got her into trouble. If only she hadn't chased me. If only she hadn't yelled her beak off, *Wisp! I'm coming with you!*

Instead of turning back and rushing to her rescue, here I am flying away from her as fast as my wings will take me.

But maybe it's okay. She's got Mom to defend her. She'll be fine. It's me the Guardians want, not her.

Oh, I don't know. Poor Willo. What will they do to her? It's all my fault.

My thoughts flip-flop like this until drowned out by hunger.

I've been flying all day and night up the Coco river, angling due north through the rainforest. How does a navigational moron like me know this? Except for the Willo thing, all is going according to plan.

Find the same river that I followed to the Refugium last fall, the one a kingfisher told me flowed due south. *Check.*

Fly fast and low, tucked out of sight along the riverbank. *Check.*

Keep going until you have *totally* run out of fuel and have to stop for a hunting break. *Check.*

That's now.

I haven't eaten since the morning of my escape—maybe a dozen fire ants and a dung beetle. *Yuck.* In spite of all the scrumptious bugs whizzing past me over the river, I wasn't about to risk chasing them until I knew I was in the clear.

That's here.

There's no way anybody could find me this far from the Refugium.

I catch the clatter of beetle wings. I lunge after the sound, dropping to just a feather's width above the river. There! A huge longhorn beetle zigzags over the water in a whirl of glossy green wings.

I trim my feathers for a burst of speed. I snap up the beetle and crunch it down in one sweet gulp.

I climb above the water and cruise beside the riverbank, looking for dessert. My shadow startles a flock of macaws. They explode in a cloud of red and green feathers. A fat blue butterfly trails after them. I scoop it up in one lightning swoop.

What easy pickings! Five minutes of hunting for a day's worth of food. Not like those suckers in the Refugium. I shudder in midair just thinking about that horrible place.

As if in response to my thoughts, the First Oath starts reciting itself in my head. *Blessed be our winter Refugium, for it saves us from all perils and hunger.*

"Hah!" I say out loud, surprised I can even remember it.

Let the rest of the Colony hide deep in the suffocating jungle. Let them peck away at the soggy ground like barnyard chickens while I pluck the juiciest bugs out of the sunlit air.

The taste of freedom.

Then I remember Willo and feel suddenly, hopelessly exhausted.

For the first time in two days, I flare my wings, extend my feet, and land. I choose a dead tree-fern that leans out over the river.

I'm used to being invisible. Getting pretty good at it. My brown and white feathers blend perfectly with the tree-fern's dry fronds. I feel safe here, hidden from crawling or leaping things that like to eat birds. And from the probing eyes of Guardians.

Just a little nap and I'm outta here.

So what if it's a few weeks before the rest of the Colony starts the North Crossing? Who needs them? That's when I feel the Second Oath rising. *Blessed be the protection and guidance of Guardians during all our Crossings, North and South.*

Correction, please. *Blessed be the last day I ever set eyes on another Guardian goon!* If all goes according to plan, that day has already come and gone.

Even as my eyes fall shut, the thought of my solo adventure from the Amazon to the Arctic sends a shiver through my wings.

I fall into a delicious dream about a treeless land buzzing with bugs. I'm chasing my high-flying father, pulling off barrel rolls, corkscrews, and booming dives. We fly like one bird, weightless and free. My eyes never stray from Dad's wings, trimmed in gold by the midnight sun.

The flutter of fidgety wings crashes into my dream. I awake with a start, tensing for an instant launch.

"Look out! Look out!" chirps a chatty blue manakin whose tree I've apparently stolen.

I relax my wings. "What?" I groan watching the little bird flit before me, her pouting beak and cherry cap all a blur.

The manakin bursts into a crazy loop-de-loop, then sets down right on my back.

"Ah, excuse me?" I say, knocking her off with a flick of a wing.

"Listen! Listen!"

Off in the distance, I hear deep-throated bellows and

heaving croaks as if a dozen howler monkeys are throwing up all at once. "You mean *that*?"

"No, listen!"

Above the sloshing river, I hear a low coughing sound in the jungle that makes my neck feathers bristle.

I shove my head through the fronds and look down.

A pudu deer leaps out of the jungle and onto a patch of riverside mud. She takes a few nervous glances back at the jungle and inches onto the mud. Her black and white tail twitches as she sniffs the air.

I peer behind the deer at a palm leaf that shouldn't be shaking.

The jungle seems to hold its breath.

"Too late! Too late!" the manakin cries and she drops from the tree, zooming straight for the deer.

I spot a flash of orange.

Before I got trapped in the Refugium, I'd learned a lot about life and death in the rainforest. That coughing sound can mean only one thing.

With the manakin fluttering madly about its ears, the deer tries to yank its legs out of the sucking mud. Bright red butterflies scatter above its head. A howler monkey belches an alarm.

A jaguar springs out of the forest like a bat from a cave. It pounces on the deer, flattening it against the mud. The deer squeals and rakes her antlers behind her, trying to stab the jaguar's face. The jaguar sinks its fangs into the deer's neck, gives it a wicked shake, then crunches the life out of her.

The manakin dive-bombs the jaguar over and over, pecking its spotted ears.

Brave little twit.

The jaguar suddenly leaps up and swipes at the bird with both forelegs, missing it by a claw-length.

The manakin zips into the jungle, trailed by a roar so loud it sends shivers up my tree and down my neck.

The giant cat settles back to its meal. I close my eyes to the spreading carpet of blood. Above the crunching of bones I hear the river calling me back to sleep. *Another quick nap and I'll be good to go.*

For an instant, the jaguar glows in my head like it's made of … stars … until I drop into a deep and dreamless sleep.

The attack comes without warning. Not from below but above.

I stir to a tiny tremor rippling the dry fronds around me. Before I can open my eyes, a ring of hairy legs clamps on to my head.

The attacker squeezes my skull, injecting white-hot needles into my eyes, my brain. I thrash my wings, trying to beat off the unseen terror.

The brittle fronds collapse beneath me.

I drop from the tree-fern, unable to fly.

Blinded by the hairy thing locked on my head, I land with a thud in the blood-soaked mud.

5

FLYING BLIND

Coco River, Ecuador rainforest

I feel my bowels open as I thrash against whoever's clamped on my head. Blood and mud splash into my beak.

Thwack!

A paw slams down on my tail.

Long whiskers sweep across my belly.

The hairy beast on my head makes a weird hissing noise.

The jaguar lifts its paw.

I pry my wings off the mud and bolt.

The jaguar's roar almost knocks me out of the air.

Blinded by needles in my brain, I barely know up from down. But I can tell my attacker's grip is weakening. Where once there were eight legs crushing my head, now there are only three. I feel my attacker's body swaying under me as I dip and twirl, trying to shake the horrible thing off.

"Wisp!"

Who the—? "Get this off me!"

"Wisp! You're going to crash into the jungle! Go back to the river!"

I hear the staccato flap of nighthawk wings above me. "Willo? How did you—"

"Go back!"

"I can't see! Which way?"

"Follow my voice!"

I flip into a couple of barrel-rolls.

Another leg slips from my head. *Only two to go.*

"Good, Wisp! You almost dumped him! God, he's ugly!"

"Who? What?" I try another barrel-roll but the thing just digs in, spreading fire deeper into my brain.

"NO!" Willo screams. "Over here! You almost hit a tree!"

"What's on my head?"

"Pull up! The river!"

"But I thought you said—"

"Not *in* the river! Pull up!"

I've got only one trick left. Go up.

"What are you *doing*?" Willo shouts.

I can't answer. I save every breath for the climb.

Higher and higher.

Flames scorch my brain, my flight muscles.

Higher yet.

Willo spins around me as I claw the air for height. "Are you nuts? How do you expect to—"

A thunder in my ears drowns out her voice. When I feel

my body will burst, I tuck both wings and roll into a blind, deadweight dive.

I accelerate to what Dad once called "terminal velocity," the fastest a falling bird can go. At this speed, I can only guess where the river might be. Too late and I'm dead.

Now!

I flare my wings and jerk out of the dive. As I'd hoped, the force is too much for my attacker and, with one last rake across my skull, it lets go.

That same weird hissing noise fills the air until swallowed by a hollow plop.

The fire in my brain dies down. Light returns to my eyes. I can make out a fuzzy wash of sky blue and jungle green. Things are looking up until I spread my wings, snap into an uncontrolled stall, and smash into the river.

"Wisp! Get out of there!"

For a moment, I float half-dead on my back, vaguely aware of crazy splashing all around me.

"Fly! Piranhas!"

Terror floods my veins and I shoot out of the water.

"So where did you learn to fly like that?" Willo asks.

"Which part, exactly?" My vision is returning and I can dimly make out Willo seesawing through the air in front of me. I have to concentrate hard to avoid crashing into trees that poke out of the jungle like monster mushrooms.

"Like, when you flew upside down with a spider on your head?"

"A spider?"

"A Goliath bird-eating spider, actually."

"Goliath?"

"Honest. Arwen's always trying to creep us out about them."

This is news to me. I never listened to Arwen. But Willo eats up this kind of stuff.

"That thing saved your life when it hissed. Spooked the jaguar."

"A hissing spider?"

"Yep. Arwen says it even shoots out evil hairs."

"She's right about that, at least." I do a quick barrel-roll to shake out the last needles of pain smoldering in my head.

"Who taught you that?" Willo asks.

"Barrel-roll," I say, flipping into another. "Learned it from an Arctic tern on the way down. You just tuck in one wing like this and—"

"Nighthawks don't fly like that!"

"Dad did."

"Maybe, but Mom never let him teach you that stuff."

There she goes again, picking on Dad. I think she's jealous of what we had. "Look, can we just keep Dad out of this? What I need to know is how you found me."

"I had to work pretty hard. At least you could've waited."

"I don't recall inviting you."

"I remember things, like when you told Mom and me about following this river to the Refugium."

What a blunder that was.

"Seemed like a no-brainer that you'd just follow it back north. Good you were zonked out or I never would've caught up."

Mental note: no more napping. "Did you tell anyone else?"

"Yeah, sure, with a bunch of goons on my back?"

"How'd you bust out?" I'm secretly a little proud of her for that.

"Same as you. Through that crack. Got stuck in there. The spider monkeys sat on me until the Guardians took off. Then they yanked me out."

"They didn't follow you?"

"The monkeys?"

"Agh! The Guardians!"

"Don't see any, do you?"

I peer over both shoulders. Still half-blind, I try to make sense of the smears of color around me. That's when I notice we're nowhere near the river. "Hey! Where are you leading me?"

"Back to the Refugium, of course."

I snap into a hover. "The Refugium!"

"Just for another few weeks. Till we start the North Crossing."

"*Weeks!* I'd suffocate in there. Besides, they'd throw us both in the Hutch for sure."

"Oh. I forgot about that."

I bank steeply away from her.

"Wait! I'm coming with you!"

I tuck my wings and drop back to the river "Get down! They'll see you!"

"We're good, Wisp! No one followed me!"

My sister. So smart to find me. So dumb to think Flare isn't tailing her, that she's not leading him right to me.

I tuck back out of sight along the riverbank, praying I won't crash into anything with my wonky vision.

"Wisp! Wait up!"

Thanks for saving me, Willo, but I'm outta here.

I set my wings for maximum thrust.

I'll shake her off my tail; she beetles back to the Refugium; Mom protects her from those nasty Guardians; and my solo adventure is back on track.

Then I remember. *Mom knows.*

Willo's words boom back to me. *You told Mom and me about following this river* ... They'll interrogate her, for sure. Maybe even torture her. Peck her brain until she talks. Then again, maybe she'll *want* to tell them. She'll want a goon squad sent out to fetch her little darlings home.

Back to the Refugium.

Either way, I'm sunk.

6

GIANT RAVEN
Columbia rainforest

Thousands of wingbeats north, I steal a glance over my shoulder. Squinting, I can just make out a lone nighthawk ducking in and out of the riverside jungle, struggling to keep up.

Almost as fast as me. Dad was always a speed demon. Must run in the family.

I break into a wide circle over the river and grudgingly wait for Willo. When she's just a few wingbeats from me, I scoot away. I don't want to give her any sign that I might be softening, that I'm actually glad for her company.

Which I definitely am not.

To be honest, for all the planning and dreaming I did for this journey, I hadn't given any thought to what happens when the Coco River runs out. I knew that, direction-wise,

I'd be good as long as I could follow it. But as the river gets narrower and shallower, starts winding into the hills, I'm thinking, *Goodbye, Coco. Hello, confusion.*

Luckily the rainforest carries on so I'll have lots of cover if I need to hide. In the meantime, my plan is to skim the jungle treetops, stay low and fast, not stop until I'm three-quarters dead.

Whatever it takes to ditch Flare and his goons.

Willo pants up beside me. "Why didn't you follow me?" she says in that trying voice of hers.

"I don't follow anybody."

"Then at least you could wait for me."

"You wanted to go back to the Refugium. Who am I to stop you?"

"Where are we going, anyway?"

"Who's *we*?"

"Okay, you."

"None of your business."

"Yellowknife?"

"Not exactly. Farther."

"What do you mean?"

"The Tundra."

Willo lurches toward the river like I have avian flu. "Don't say that!"

"Tundra, Tundra, Tundra! What's your problem?"

"You know nighthawks can't fly there."

"Watch me ... On second thought, *don't* watch me. Instead, why don't you just fly back to Mommy. Think how worried she must—"

"What about the Third Oath? You know, like, there's nothing beyond the Boreal, just rock and ice."

"How would you know?"

"That's what everybody says."

"Dad wasn't everybody."

"We were just chicks. He made up those stories."

"Nope. A snow goose told me about it. They nest on the Tundra. On huge green plains humming with bugs, just like Dad said."

"You hang out with *snow geese*?"

"Why not?" I extend my wings and rock from side to side, eyes half-closed. "Ever tried flying in a v-shaped flock? It's incredible. Hardly any wind resistance. You can cruise for hours without—"

"Okay, so you believe Dad's giant raven story, too?"

My wings skip a beat. Willo has hit the one story that stalks me at night. That I've wrestled with till my head hurts. The one story that takes the shine off my Tundra dream.

The giant raven.

I think of Willo and me, barely fledglings, tucked together on the school's pebble roof, Dad perched on the poplar branch where he liked to tell us stories. I can almost hear his voice ...

Once there was a giant raven that lived alone on the Tundra. It was so big it blotted out the stars when it flew. It was so terrifying, no bird could live within a hundred million wingbeats of it and hope to survive. When it cried out, its woeful voice shook the whole Tundra as if with the sound of thunder. No one knew that the giant raven was actually lonely. That he was the last of a great race of ravens that once ruled the Arctic. No one knew this except for the silver-winged birds that, to this day, live among his impossibly black feathers.

I guess the fact that this story still scares me silly says that maybe I believe it. No Arctic birds I've met have ever talked about a giant raven. But Dad got all his stories from the stars and, as he always told us, *Stars can't lie*. There must be some kind of truth to it. I don't know what. "For sure, I believe it," I say, hoping this might scare off Willo.

"That story's just frog feathers. Slow down, will you. Mom'll be fine. I'm coming with you."

7

INFERNO
Columbia rainforest

I'd never admit it, but Willo actually proves useful once we leave the Coco's headwaters. From what I'd learned about the South Crossing while stuck in the Refugium, once we're out of the rainforest, the fastest flyway bends northwest toward the Andes Mountains. Hard to hide a mountain chain but, remember, I don't have a clue about directions.

Of course, I can't let on to Willo about this, so I'm wondering how I'm going to find northwest without revealing my secret. Then I get a brainwave. Just catch some serious height, spot the mountains, and go for it.

Brilliant idea, Wisp. Spiral up into the open and any Guardians would spot us for sure.

I decide to switch to the most sophisticated navigational trick I know.

Ask directions.

Trouble is, there's nobody to ask. The rainforest has been eerily silent for the last few thousand wingbeats. Any birds we do see are streaming south in mixed flocks—parrots flying with macaws, umbrella birds with toucans. Weird. It's like they're fleeing from something.

I find out soon enough what that is.

At first I think it's my eyes, still fuzzy, thanks to that horrible spider. There's a gray gloom over everything and the sky ahead is all smudgy.

I wrack my brain to figure out which way to go.

Nothing comes.

I've got to ask somebody. But who? How can I, with Willo leeching onto me?

Willo.

Why not ask her? But I have to be sly. Make it a game. "So … uh, I bet you can't guess where east is."

"What?"

"Due east. Bet you can't point to it."

"Can so," she says and shoots away at an angle in front of my right wing.

Oops. That tells me we're actually headed northeast. "Okay, how about … southwest?"

She shoots out straight behind us. *That confirms it.*

"Okay, your turn," she says as she circles back to my side.

I clench my beak. I hadn't thought about this part of the game.

"How about … northwest," she says playfully.

I've been struggling to store these simple bearings in my

head. My mind goes into a tailspin. My heart starts to race. I get dizzy and can barely distinguish up from down, ahead from behind.

I close my eyes, wanting to end this stupid game, this ridiculous adventure to the Tundra. What a fool I was to think I could pull it off alone. A navigational nincompoop.

"Are you all right, Wisp?"

I open my eyes and turn my head a bit left. *At least she'll tell me if I goof up.* I pump my wings and shoot off in that direction. "Northwest it is!" I shout. Dad once told me: *Make your mistakes big and loud. You'll learn more from them.*

I circle back to Willo, holding my breath.

She seems distracted. "Can you smell it, Wisp?"

"Northwest? Well, a blue jay told me that he could actually navigate by—"

"No, goof. Smoke."

Willo has a way better sense of smell than me. I take a big sniff. Only a hint of kapok flowers. "Of course I can smell it."

She's looking in the exact direction I just flew. I squint, half-hoping it's still my wonky eyes.

It's not my eyes.

The sky ahead is much darker. Smoke curls from horizon to horizon. Here and there, it flashes orange or coils upward like a snake ready to strike.

"No wonder those birds were screaming out of here," I say. I look down at the rainforest canopy and spot several rivers of spider monkeys, all headed in the same direction. Away from the smoke.

"Why go northwest if we don't have to?"

At least I got that right. Maybe there's hope yet. "We have to."

"What about ducking into the rainforest and waiting it out?"

"I'm not stopping till we're over the mountains. You can turn back anytime."

"Forget it. But can't we just fly *over* the smoke?"

I tip my head up. My beak drops open. The smoky curtain reaches as high as the highest thunderhead I've ever seen. "And put on a nice little sky dance for any Guardians chasing us? Hey, goons! Come and get us! Uh ... I don't think so. Could even be ice crystals way up there."

"Yeah, but just *look* at it. There's no way we can ..." Willo's voice breaks off into a tremble.

"We'll stay low like always. How big can it be?"

Very big, it turns out.

The Yellowknife fire was big but nothing like this. The scariest part about that fire was its speed. How fast it ate half the town. I'd seen some other big fires up north but always from a great height, not barreling straight into them. I once met an olive-sided flycatcher who knew a lot about forest fires. He told me the trick is to stay above the flames and below the smoke. "Aim for that sweet spot," he'd said. "Then you can fly through anything."

Never tried it myself but that's all I have to go on. My backup plan is to find a pond or something. If things get really crazy in there, we can ditch into the water.

As we get closer to the fire, the sound of exploding trees is almost deafening.

"Just stay on my tail!" I yell.

"Wisp, this is *nuts!*"

"Turn back then! I'm going in!"

She doesn't turn back. *Looks like she's in this for the long haul.*

It's like flying through hot gray muck. I try descending but the heat becomes unbearable. I try ascending but the smoke becomes unbreathable. I'm starting to doubt my own sanity when I see a thin layer of clear air ahead, broken by flaming trees.

The sweet spot.

With flames reaching for me from all sides, I'm afraid to look behind. "Willo! Still there?"

Just the roar of fire and crashing trees.

"Willo!"

More explosions and what sounds like the death scream of a howler monkey.

I risk a glance over my shoulder. No Willo. Smoke closes in all around me. Above the chaos of the fire, I hear another kind of roar.

Can it be?

I desperately scan the burning carpet below me and spot a dark gash that maybe, just maybe, is rushing water. I hold my breath and swoop down to it.

What the...

I spot a nighthawk perched on a rock sticking out of a wide frothy stream.

"I think we're good here for a while!" Willo yells.

I'm as relieved as I am angry. "I told you to stay behind me!"

"You told me to look for water if things got crazy! Seemed like the perfect—"

Willo's words are swallowed by more explosions and the

thumping of fallen trees. "Is this crazy enough for you?" she yells.

I look upstream, which, from this angle, looks like molten lava. I discover we are not alone. Standing up to their bellies in water, framed against a towering wall of fire, is a family of tapirs, a jaguar, and a deer like the one I saw get ripped apart by, yes, a jaguar.

"We can't stay here," I say.

"Why not?" Willo says, pointing a wing at all the animals. "They look safe enough."

A coil of flaming vines drops smack on one of the smaller tapirs. Its pitiful squeal pierces even the fire's roar.

"They can't fly!" I yell. "Let's go!"

All kinds of flaming foliage sail past us and go fizzing into the water as we follow the stream through the inferno. After several near hits with burning trees, more fire bombs, and a tree sloth dangling by one toe, I sense a thinning of the smoke and flames. I spot what looks like a distant human, all wiggly in the heat waves, moving about while beating something against a patch of sunlit ground.

"We're gonna make it!" I yell. "We're gonna—"

I feel a searing pain on my right wing as it takes a direct hit from a falling ember.

"Wisp!"

I tumble sideways and land beak first in the churning stream.

8

FLARE
Coco River, Ecuador rainforest

"Skim the treetops. Stay low. Don't let him see us!"

Flare barks commands to his diamond-shaped flock of Guardians.

After the double breakout of Wisp and Willo, Flare had convinced Arwen that he was ready to lead a Guardian search party to capture and punish them. Arwen had promised to promote him to Principal Guardian if he succeeded in this mission. *What I've wanted forever!* Flare had thought as he bowed low to his Queen. *My father's rank, supreme leader of all Guardians. But my father groveled before indigo wingbars. Not me. After this mission, look out, Chickie. It's gilded all the way.*

"If you fail," Arwen had told him, as if reading his thoughts, "your gilded wingbar feathers will be plucked out by the quills and you will be thrown to the Plebeian throng."

Hatched into the highest class of Guardians and endowed with remarkable size and strength, Flare had never known failure. And now, granted command over the most powerful and highly trained squadron in the Colony, he knew this mission would be no exception.

"My squadron," he'd told Arwen, "could find a dust mite in a blizzard."

Before launching, Flare conducted what he'd called a "lively chat" in the Hutch with Fern, his enemy's mother. He'd emerged from the Hutch alone, knowing exactly where to start his hunt.

The Coco River.

Flare drops like a stone over a row of tall palm trees and the river rushes up to him.

"Fan out! Dragnet formation! Search both riverbanks!"

Flare falls into slow zigzag sweeps a mere feather-width above the river.

At the back of the flock, Hammer, bravest and strongest of Flare's Guardians, echoes his leader's every movement. The rest of the squadron forms an aerial net that arcs up from the water to the highest tree, allowing them to scour the jungle edge for any delinquent nighthawks that might be hiding there.

They fly like this until Flare hears a shout from Striker, his Chief Investigator, who has set down below a dead tree-fern that leans out over the river. Flare steers his squadron back to him and they land on a wide strip of riverside mud.

"Careful, sir," Striker says.

"Don't *careful* me, Striker. What did you find?"

"If you'd just step back a bit, sir."

Flare grunts and hops backwards.

Striker points a wing at a spray of whitish mud. "Look, sir."

"Bird shit. Excellent, Striker. What of it?"

"Nighthawk, sir. And here, its wingprints and tracks." Striker waves a wing over a jumble of paw prints. "And a jaguar, sir. Big one."

Flare scratches the mud with one of his slashing claws. Blood oozes up. "Hmm. One dead nighthawk. I'd hoped to witness that myself."

"We can't be sure, sir. Not enough feathers here to suggest a bird kill. I suspect this blood is from another source." Striker points a wing at a jumble of fresh bones sticking out of the water downstream. "Could be a deer or a tapir."

Flare scoops a red dragonfly off a leaf floating by and angrily crunches it down. "Well then, we'll just have to continue upriver until we find that rat, won't we."

"Yes, sir."

As his squadron lifts off, Flare hears a sudden splash behind him. He glances over his shoulder just in time to see Hammer disappear down the throat of a big toothy caiman.

"*Drack-ack-ack-ack!*" he curses.

Flare wheels back and circles above a ring of seething bubbles. His squadron buzzes around him in disarray.

He shoots away from the water, yelling, "What are you staring at? Resume diamond formation! Move it!"

Something boils over inside Flare as he strains for more speed with his muscle-bound wings. "*Wisp!*" he screams to the silent jungle. "Plebeian scum! You will pay dearly for this!"

9

THE ITCH
Northern plains of Columbia

It's the stream that saves me. Spits me out of the flaming rainforest into a smoldering wasteland of fallen trees. Several humans are working here, big ones, little ones, all bent over, slashing at stumps, yanking on logs, clearing away the charred remains of what once was teeming rainforest.

Everyone's absorbed in their work and I drift right past them, too weak to do anything but lift my beak above the ash-choked water.

"Wisp!"

The voice that so often makes me cringe now lifts me almost clear out of the stream. "Willo! Where are you?"

"Right above you, goof. Get out of there! You're headed for a waterfall!"

Above the muffled forest fire, I can hear the crash of

falling water just downstream. I try to launch but my wings are too wet and wounded. I try to flail upstream but—too late—I'm over the edge and spinning through the air.

"Fly!" yells Willo.

In spite of the searing pain in my right wing, I catch some lift before I'm smothered by falling water or beaned by a tumbling log. I have to rest, someplace, but the ground is still glowing here and there from the fire. I aim for the closest thing that looks safe.

An old brown cow, standing in a mud puddle. It hardly looks up when I land on its back.

"What are you doing?" Willo says, circling above me.

"Come on," I call back, suddenly feeling giddy just to be alive. "We're going to hitch a ride to the Andes!"

With the rainforest now far behind us, we fly over a broad, rolling savannah dotted with palm trees, banana plantations, and cattle. Up ahead, a wall of sawtooth mountains pokes up into the morning sun.

The Andes.

Through a bunch of roundabout questions, I've learned from Willo that our main flyway follows some kind of mountain pass through there. The farther north we go, the more I depend on her for this kind of info. And, sly as I am, the more she seems to know it.

"Still there?" I shout, without looking back.

"Yeah, I'm good," Willo says, barely able to get her words out between gasps. "Till those mountains, anyway."

"Tuck in closer. It's half the work. Like a snow goose, remember? Works better in a v, but I guess that's hard to make with just two birds."

Willo tries to laugh but it comes out as a desperate wheeze.

I shake my head.

It was sitting on that cow, inspecting each other's feathers after the fire, when I realized that she was way worse off than me. My right wing got scorched and it stung like heck. But Willo? Somehow she'd bashed up her tail feathers, chasing after me through the fire. Now here I am on a billion wingbeat journey with a sister who can barely steer.

Funnily enough, she's the one who has any sense of direction.

"I'm hungry!" she cries.

"You just pigged out on grasshoppers back in that bean field."

"I'm *still* hungry!"

"Could you maybe focus on flying, for a change?"

"Do you really think we can get over those mountains? I mean, with my feathers like this?"

"No problem."

"Are you *sure* this is the right way?"

You're the one that pointed us here. "Stop asking me that!"

My head floods with questions. What landmarks will guide us? What's the safest time to travel? What's the quickest route north?

I don't know.

Then comes the question that vexes me most. *Is the Tundra even real?*

Of course it is. I heard Dad's stories. I saw the sparkle in his eyes, heard the thrill in his voice. But is that all they were? *Stories?* Were those snow geese kidding me?

I shake the racket from my head.

Just trust in the same instinct or gut feeling or plain luck that led me straight to the Refugium weeks after the rest of the Colony arrived.

I showed them.

They can call me a vagrant.

I'm free.

My bravado lasts a few wingbeats, then fades like mist in a whirlwind. As the mountains ahead grow taller, sharper, I get this sick feeling that the unmarked flyway ahead, reaching across two continents, is booby-trapped with an evil chain of storms, starvation, predators, and death.

I swallow hard, fixing my eyes on the highest mountain peak. I trim my wings and boost my pace.

Somehow I'd guessed my way south and survived. Bless the winds, I can do it again in reverse.

I glance back at Willo who beats furiously to catch up.

"Hey! Wait up!" she yells.

I ease back to half my normal cruising speed. "Okay, okay."

I had thought the burning itch would go away once I started north.

I was wrong.

It's only getting worse.

Adding to the nagging tug of the Tundra is a new crying need that comes as a complete surprise. Here I'd stuck my neck out so many times to be alone. Now comes this new itch. The itch for companionship—but definitely not of the sisterly kind.

10

BLACKFIN
Foothills of the Andes Mountains, Columbia

My head spins with worries and doubt. I cringe at the sound of Willo's panting behind me, getting harsher with each wingbeat. I wonder if I'm pushing her too hard even at this slug pace. I kid myself that I'm still in charge of where and when we stop, let alone where we're headed.

"Wisp ... Wi-i-i-sp ... I'm pooped!"

I stare harder at the fishtail peak that's pulled us clear across the savannah. Blackfin Mountain. That's what Willo called it, anyway. Never seen it myself. Without me asking directions, Willo had given me something solid to aim for. I could still look like I actually knew where I was going.

She'd told me that, on the South Crossing, a lot of the

Colony, even some Guardians, cheered or broke down crying once they'd safely passed this mountain. I'm about to find out why.

"Wisp!"

"What?" *As if I didn't know.*

We're finally entering the Andes Mountains, one of the deadliest legs of our journey. Or so a golden plover told me last fall. His words fly back to me now, impaling my brain. "More birds bite it through the Andes than the rest of the trip combined," he'd said as we breezed over the Gulf of Mexico. That's why I'd stuck with his flock and detoured east over Venezuela, what he'd called "the scenic route."

But we don't have time for that now. Not with Flare and his goons on our tails.

This will be my first mountain crossing and I can't wait to get it behind us. Willo's timing is perfectly awful.

"I can't, Wisp ... I really can't go any further ... Just a little nap ... Maybe some more grasshoppers ... a few ants, even..."

I dart a glance over my shoulder. Willo trails far behind me, losing altitude, slipping fast toward the stony foothills far below.

For the first time in hours, I break my arrow's path for Blackfin Mountain. Steaming inside, I dip one wing and circle back to my little sister's side. "All right, already." A tremor in my stomach says that I, too, could use a bug refill before tackling the peaks ahead.

I scan the foothills and pick a bright green lake perched on a ledge halfway up the mountain. "Down there. A quick lunch stop, then we go over the top."

Willo nods weakly.

We pull in our wings and plunge into a meadow of high grass rimming the lake.

I have to admit it feels good to fold my weary wings. Sleep ambushes us before we say a word.

I wake to a horsey snort. I look at Willo.

Still dead to the world.

I blast out of the grass and startle a small herd of pointy-eared alpacas dopily chewing their cud in the late afternoon sun.

Late afternoon.

I thwack my wings against the thin mountain air. *Curse the winds! We slept too long!*

I unwind a notch. No matter. We're nighthawks. We rule the night.

There I go, wavering again.

I lift my beak to Blackfin's summit, now wearing a tuft of cloud, first I've seen all day. Not a good sign.

That settles it. We go while the weather holds.

I drop toward Willo who is still asleep. Nestled in the thick dry grass, she is practically invisible. My little sister is safe. She is warm. Thinking about what might lie ahead of us, I want to stretch this moment on and on. Instead, I hover above her head and flood her with serious gusts of wing-wash. "Get up! We gotta go!"

"I'm starved," she whines. "Supposed to be a lunch stop, remember?"

"More like supper."

Willo breaks into impish laughter.

"What?"

"Your head."

"What about it?"

"Looks like you got chewed on by termites."

"Spider claws, actually. Oh, yeah, and a little forest fire. You should talk. With those tail feathers, it looks like you got sat on by a cow."

We share a few seconds of sibling comfort with a good laugh.

"Look," I say, suddenly sounding like my father. "It'll be dark soon, so we don't have time to fool around before we hit the mountains."

"Wait, we're going over *tonight*? You don't even know where we're going!"

"Do so."

"Okay, but what's there to eat in the mountains? What if we get caught in a storm? What if we—"

"Enough stupid questions. We're wasting time."

Willo shuffles from one foot to the other. "I say we fly back to the Refugium and take our chances."

I lift my wings for takeoff. "Go if you like."

Willo clenches her beak and scrunches her eyes.

I hate when she does that. "Your choice, Willo, the Hutch or freedom?"

Her eyes pop open. "Let's eat."

We launch into the air, causing a stir among the alpacas. They trot away, casting dirty looks at us over their shoulders. We skim low over the still lake, scooping freshly hatched stoneflies off the glassy surface.

I'm relieved to see how well my beat-up sister can still dive after bugs. She may not be fast and her steering is off, but at least she can feed herself.

As we spiral up into the chilled mountain air, I feel a sudden release of tension. I thrill to the certainty that every wingbeat brings me closer to the land of the midnight sun and my own private freedom. Nothing, not these mountains, not darkness, not even my little sister can stop me now.

These sunny thoughts lift me over Blackfin Mountain but quickly dry up and blow away when I see what lies beyond.

11

THE THROAT
Andes Mountains, Columbia

The sky turns on us the moment we clear Blackfin's peak. We fly side by side, struggling to keep our balance in the thin air and a rising tailwind that wants to knock us out of the sky.

"I remem ... place," Willo shouts, her words shredded by the wind.

"What?"

"This place. I remember it. Mom called it the Thro ..."

"Throat?"

"Yeah. Just look at it."

At first I see only jagged mountains. Then it all falls into place. The teeth, a tight semicircle of pointy peaks even higher than Blackfin. The tongue, a sprawling glacier that covers the valley floor. The gullet, a narrow gorge flanked by a pair of lower peaks that curve toward each other. And behind that, a huge storm cloud so black it makes a moonless night look like day.

"That cloud could eat us alive," I shout.

"It looks really hungry, Wisp."

I glance up at the ring of peaks, still thousands of wingbeats above us. "We'll have to go around it."

"Can't."

"Says who?"

"Mom. Air's too thin up there. Can't fly. Can't breathe."

"Then we'll just have to wait out the storm on the glacier," I say, trying to sound decisive. "That cloud's got to—"

"Too cold. Mom said there's weird winds down there that'll turn you to ice in no time. Besides, what are you going to eat, snow fleas?"

My stomach shrinks. All my instincts rebel. The migratory itch to push on boils my guts. But I have no choice. "Then I guess we'll have to ... turn back."

"Back to the Refugium?"

"Curse the winds, no! Just to that lake. We can wait there."

I reluctantly flare my wings and circle around into the wind.

Smack!

It's like flying full speed into a tree trunk.

What was a tricky tailwind seconds ago is now a ferocious headwind that scatters us like moths in a hurricane.

"Stick with me!" I yell as I watch Willo disappear into a backdrop of naked rock, snow, and ice.

I give chase, locking on to her angled flight path into the wind. I'm surprised how much easier it is until I remember the yellow-billed loon who taught me this trick.

"Like a fish ferrying upstream," he'd said as we battled a southerly headwind over Lake Superior. "Half the work, twice the fun."

Right now, I don't know about the fun part but it's definitely less work. The extra lift gives me an idea.

"I think this is do-able," I shout when I finally zoom up to her.

"I think this is *crazy!* We can't go back! Can't go forward! Can't go down! What do we do, Wisp?"

"Cool it, will you? We'll go up and over."

"But Mom said—"

"We're pretty high already. How much worse can it get?"

"Yeah, but—"

"Just stay at this angle. Ferry into the wind. Once we clear those peaks, we can turn downwind again and sail right past that nasty cloud."

We climb and climb into thin air. My lungs, even when filled to bursting, strain for air. My wings feel like soggy leaves. My head is ready to pop. My eyes hurt from the blinding light thrown off peaks on fire in the setting sun.

I fix my mind on one goal. *Avoid that cloud at all cost.* This seems to soften the icy wind, the searing pain in my lungs, the hungry hole in my stomach.

Mom was wrong. I can handle this.

Too bad Willo can't.

"Wisp!"

"Come on, Willo," I gasp, "You can do this! We're almost over!"

"It's no use, Wisp ... no feathers ... no muscles ... no air."

"I'll slow down for you!"

"Can't."

My favorite word.

Willo loses her grip on the magic angle that allowed us to ferry upwind. Her wings go limp and she instantly slips downwind almost crashing into a fang-shaped lump of snow.

Just a few more wingbeats and we would have been over the ring of sawtooth peaks and safely scooting around the storm cloud.

Instead, we're streaking out of control, straight for it.

I like speed but this is insane!

The cloud seems to suck all the world's air into itself. Frosty tentacles reach out and yank us into its black core.

An ear-popping roar makes communicating impossible. I have no energy for it anyway. I put all I've got into keeping my wings stable and Willo in sight.

The cloud swallows Willo first. She goes in upside down and sideways.

Wow, not bad, Willo! Where'd you learn that trick? Then I realize she's totally out of control.

I draw in my wings and brace for collision.

Thwack! I pierce the fringe of the storm cloud. Spikes of shattered snow blast my face. A wicked turbulence knocks all air from my chest. One moment, my wings bite firmly into pockets of cold hard air. The next, I'm thrown off balance as the air thins and collapses beneath my worn-out wings. It's all I can do to stay aloft.

The craziness ends as quickly as it starts. I am spit out into a dark void.

What the ...

The smell of pulverized rock hovers in the still air. The wind's eerie whine echoes all around. I look up at a swirling mass of clouds. I detect a feeble glow above it, the last trace of daylight. Swallowed whole by the Throat, I feel trapped in a bubble, spinning deep inside the rumbling stomach of a monster.

"Willo! *Queek-queek! Queek-queek!* Willo!"

My calls are answered only by the whining wind.

"Willo!"

I desperately search for my sister. I fly in an ever-wider spiral until one wingtip slams into the edge of the wild dark storm.

You'll never find her.

I *will* find her, I think. She must've been thrown in here just like me.

"Willo!"

Then, to my total amazement, she answers.

"Over here!"

I squint. Everything blurs into gray and black.

"Where?"

"Right behind you! Stop spinning around!"

"You scared me!" I would have wrapped my wings around her if we had any place to set down.

Which we don't.

"We did it, Wisp!" Willo says, sounding awfully cheery. "We got through the Throat alive!"

She doesn't know. "Look, uh, Willo. Actually we're only—"

"We'll just find a nice roost, and then—"

"We're only halfway through this thing, Willo. This is the eye of the storm."

Willo stops flapping for a second but makes a quick recovery. "Well ... it's not so bad here. Least you can fly half-straight. Kind of chilly, though."

Even in the dying light, I can see Willo's beak shaking.

"It should blow over soon, eh, Wisp?"

"We can't wait it out here," I say, noticing the shiver in my own voice. "Storm's all around us. No place to land."

This does not sit well with Willo. "But I'm starving! Freezing!"

That's when I feel icy claws grabbing my own flesh. "There's only one way out, Willo."

"Where?"

"Dive back in. Follow me!"

12

CLUES
Andes Mountains, Columbia

"They set down here, for sure."

"How can you be so sure, sir?" Striker asks.

Flare loves it when his squadron members address him as "sir," even though he knows they have no choice. He circles above an emerald-colored lake halfway up Blackfin Mountain. Striker wings close to his side while the rest of the squadron follows in a fan-shaped search formation.

Flare flicks a wing at the fishtail peak above them. "Blackfin is a magnet for every damned bird leaving the Amazon."

"Except for ducks, sir."

Smart ass, thinks Flare. "Details, details, Striker. You want to learn something or not?"

"Of course, sir."

"Then, shut up. So, if you're high enough, you can see Blackfin a million wingbeats away. All the dickie birds headed north have to funnel through here."

"And nighthawks, too, sir."

"Not our Colony. Not anymore, if I can help it."

"Sir?"

"Later, Striker."

"But this lake, sir. What's special about it?"

"Well, tell me, how are you feeling after our non-stop flight from the Amazon?"

"A hundred percent, sir."

"Don't lie to me, Striker."

"To be honest, sir, I am feeling a bit peckish."

"Duh. This lake is the last source of bugs and water before you hit the mountain flyway. Any nighthawk in their right mind is going to set down here to refuel."

"But, sir, I understand that Wisp has little respect for customary flyways. Who says he didn't skirt these mountains altogether and fly over Venezuela?"

"*I* say!" Flare shouts. *This punk is too smart for his own good.* "Now go find me some clues to help track him!"

"Yes, sir."

Flare spots a small herd of grazing alpacas. "And send up my Chief Translator. Looks like we could use her."

"Right away, sir."

Striker zooms to the rear of the fan and passes the order to the squadron's only female member. Small even for her sex, she is hardly bigger than a lowly Plebe. Same goes for her claws and beak, though she does have the telltale gilded wingbars and larger feet of her class. Her odd features naturally make her the brunt of many jokes among the Guardian ranks. But what she lacks in size, she makes up for in speed. Her light frame and slender wings make her the nimblest flier of them all. Faster than any of the Colony's Guardians who, for all their muscle and might, are not famous for their speed.

Peevo.

"You called for me, sir?" Peevo says, as she glides up beside her commander.

Flare has never been good with Spanish, especially dealing with the funny accents of four-footed beasts. He resents his female translator almost as much as he depends on her. Peevo, Arwen's cultured pet, who got to spend last winter in Europe, learning God knows how many languages, who's seen too much of the world for Flare's liking, who could even be called diplomatic—which is pretty weird for a Guardian.

"I'm ... uh ... too busy to talk to those alpacas down there," Flare snaps. "Go ask them if they've seen a couple of nighthawks pass through here lately."

"Yes, sir."

Peevo flutters down to the lead alpaca, a large male with thick cinnamon wool and a bearing fit for a lion.

Flare circles within earshot, pretending to scan the high grass for clues of Wisp's passage.

Peevo perches on a tall boulder in front of the alpacas and bows to their leader. *"Saludos, Gran Jefe."*

The head alpaca lifts its great wooly head, freezing its lower buckteeth in mid-chew.

"What did you say?" Flare whispers gruffly.

"I said: 'Greetings, Great Chief.'"

"Fine. Get on with it."

"¿Han visto recientemente a unas aves raras?" Peevo says.

Flare blinks hard. "What?"

"What you told me, sir. Seen any strange birds lately?" Peevo looks peeved. "Shall I continue, sir?"

"Of course."

The alpaca slowly backs away. His herd skitters in behind him.

"¿Aves como nosotros?" Peevo says, pouring on the charm. "Birds like us," she whispers out of the side of her beak.

"¡Váyanse halcones!" shouts the alpaca in a garbled mountain drawl that mystifies Flare. *"¡No los queremos aquí!"*

Flare flaps over to the rock and plunks down beside Peevo. He gives the alpaca a perfunctory nod. "Well?"

"He says, 'Go away, hawks. We don't want you here.'"

Flare clenches his beak. "Tell him we're *not* hawks! Why does everybody call us that? We're nighthawks, for dirt's sake!"

"Sir?"

"Not hawks! *Night*hawks. Tell him!"

Peevo nods. *"No somos halcones. Somos chotacabras."*

The alpaca stomps the ground with his razor hoof. *"La última vez que aves como ustedes se detuvieron aquí, mi esposa embarazada se asustó y casi tuvo un aborto involuntario."*

Flare looks at Peevo, bug-eyed.

"He says that last time birds like us stopped here—"

"Last time?"

"Please, sir, let me finish. He says that his pregnant mate got scared and almost had a miscarriage."

"That's ridiculous!"

The alpaca stomps again. *"Los de tu tipo se roban a nuestros corderos. ¡Váyanse!"*

"He says that our kind steal their lambs."

Flare huffs. "What crap. Hawks? Sure. Nighthawks? Never! The biggest thing I ever ate was a rhinoceros beetle. Anything else?"

"Yes, sir. He told us to get lost."

Flare squints at the alpaca. "What does he mean, *last time*? When was that? How many birds? Go ahead, ask him! Ask him, pipsqueak!"

"La última vez? ¿Cuándo fue eso? ¿Cuántas aves?"

The alpaca keeps his eyes glued on the rest of Flare's Guardians as they swoop low over the meadow, combing it for clues. *"Dos aves. Se atrevieron a dormir en nuestro prado."*

"What, what?"

"Two birds, sir."

Flare pumps a wing. "Yes!"

"He said they dared to sleep in their meadow."

"When, when?"

"¿Cuándo, cuándo?"

The alpaca wrinkles his nose. *"Todavía puedo oler su odiosa presencia."*

"What, what?"

"He said he can still smell their hateful presence. They must have just left, sir."

"All right!" shouts Flare.

The alpaca gives Flare the evil eye, opens his mouth,

and projectile vomits a thick jet of half-digested cud all over him.

Flare bursts into the air, spraying chunky green goo from his wings. "You flea-bitten doormat!"

The alpaca lowers his long neck, flattens his ears, and snorts. The whole herd breaks into a stampede, straight for Peevo.

"*Váyanse! ¡Váyanse!*" shouts the alpaca.

"Gotcha, Chief," Peevo says. "We're leaving!" She leaps into the air, barely escaping a rain of thrashing hooves. "*Muchas gracias.*"

Flare flies straight for the lake and orders a couple of Guardians to splash water over him with their wings.

They get a bit carried away.

"Enough, enough already!"

Striker drops down to the beach with two feathers in his beak. He places them at his Commander's feet.

"What have you found, Striker?"

"Feathers, sir."

"Of course, dimwit. What do you make of them?"

Striker points to a long speckled feather with a tattered quill. "Tail feather. Plebeian nighthawk. Probably female."

"Definitely female, sir," says Peevo. "Looks like a juvenile."

Flare stoops to examine the feather. "Odd time of year for a female to molt, wouldn't you say, Peevo?"

"Agreed, sir. It's severely damaged. I suspect this bird either crashed into something or someone roughed her up along the way."

Flare nods triumphantly. "Hmm. All the better. That'll slow them down." He nudges the other feather with a fat toe as if he might catch some filthy disease. It is dark brown, tapered on one side, and shows a distinct swatch of white from the wingbar. "And this one?"

"Primary feather, sir," Striker says. "Right wing. Another juvenile Plebe. Male."

Flare's eyes close to slits. *"W-i-s-s-p."*

"It's a wonder he can fly, sir," Peevo says, studying the feather.

"Explain," Flare says.

"The tip of the feather is blackened and rough."

"Get to the point."

"Burned, sir."

Striker steps in front of Peevo as if she wasn't there. "Must have shot straight through that forest fire we flew over, sir."

Flare opens his eyes wide. "Such a pity. Why do you think he'd do something so stupid?"

"To evade you, sir," Peevo says before Striker can open his beak.

Flare nods imperceptibly, a light dawning somewhere in the darkness of his brain. "Scared and scorched, eh? Towing along his beat-up sister? I think this gives us a bit of an edge on that vagrant." He points his dagger wings to the sky. *"Kill-ree! Kill-ree!* Let's go grab him!"

13

DESCENT
Andes Mountains, Columbia

By the time we find each other on the other side of the storm cloud, it's pitch black. No moon, no stars, just a pale glow from the peaks. At first, we can only cling to the steep rock face, waiting for the wind to let up. When it finally does, we find shelter in a small cave half-plugged with snow. We cling together all night, neck to neck, panting for air.

By morning, a ring of melted snow surrounds us, made by the feeble heat lost from our bodies.

I stretch my wings and give Willo a poke in the belly.

"Aw, come on, Wisp. Just a little more sleep. I'm so-o-o tired."

"How about no. Unless you eat rocks and ice, we're outta here."

The whirling snow has changed to fog which glows yellow in the rising sun. We launch from the cave mouth and spiral up into a thick cloud that cloaks the peaks above. The mist presses in on us, damp and heavy.

We push through the cloud, wing tip to wing tip. The light brightens, promising smooth air above. My spirits rise with every gain in altitude.

"My lungs!" cries Willo.

I'm hit by the memory of Willo giving up and blowing away as we entered the mountains. I won't let this happen again. "Hang on! We're almost through!"

"Nighthawks don't fly this high!"

"Says who?"

Just before breaking free of the cloud, a sudden downdraft catches us and we plunge, twisting and helpless, back into the mist.

I'm too wasted to panic, focusing instead on simple stuff like breathing and staying airborne.

The cloud finally lets go and we pop out into full sunshine. All I can say is, "Wow!"

The air is calm. The light dazzling. Razor-sharp peaks rise like islands out of a fluffy white sea. We level off and aim for the nearest one.

We fly with open bills, gasping for air. My whole body throbs. My throat burns.

As we approach the mountaintop, the wind picks up, sending blasts of sharp ice crystals into my eyes. We set down on a bedrock shelf and quickly fall asleep in the sun, the pain draining from my body with each breath.

I awake as refreshed as could be, given my burning thirst

and gnawing hunger. I scan the sky ahead. With Willo's help—which I have totally denied so far—I'm gradually getting a grip on what due north looks like in relation to the sun, what it *feels* like. Pretty basic, I know, but that's all I'm good for.

I lift off, fixing on a distant peak that feels right. I get no peep from Willo, so either she is sleep-flying or I've got us on the right course. *All by myself.* I stick to this bearing, leading us across the endless cloud. I'm afraid to drop down until I know for sure what's below.

The cloud finally fizzles into cotton-ball tufts, revealing a chain of lush green valleys that dip away from us. I glance over my shoulder for one last look at the distant peaks, now fuzzy with mist. At that moment, I totally get why those nighthawks cried when they made it through these bird-eating mountains.

I dive.

All this crazy high altitude flight has sapped our energy and we've hardly exchanged a word all day. But Willo is pumped by our progress and breaks the silence. "Can you smell it, Wisp? The sea! The sea!"

There's Willo's better sense of smell again. "Uh ... yeah. We must be close."

We keep dropping. The air whistles past us as we zigzag down the valley to slow our descent.

At first the air is too thin to give our wings much braking power and we plunge, just barely in control. As the air pressure rises, our wings gain bite. But along with this comes a crushing pain in our ears. I decide to level off to let them adjust. I fix my eyes on a faint blue line just visible at the horizon.

"The Pacific!" shouts Willo who grabs the lead for a few wingbeats.

"Get behind me," I say. "You'll burn out before we get there."

Our lightning descent from the mountains brings us to a world amazingly different from the frozen emptiness now far behind. The air is warm and wet, giving more lift to our wings. We breathe deeply, topping up our lungs.

We dive again, now rolling with the land as it tips steeply toward the coast.

My last target for the day is a big freshwater pond at the base of a beachside cliff. We land beside it and gulp down beakfuls of cool, sweet water. We attack a thick cloud of sandflies buzzing over the pond. When our stomachs have no more room for even a flea, we nestle together on the beach against the warm cliff face.

We watch the sea's pounding surf through half-open eyes.

"We did it, eh, Wisp?"

"Yep."

"Some birds don't make it this far."

"Lots, probably."

"We're good here, eh, Wisp?"

"No snakes, anyway."

"What about at night?"

"Who cares? We fly at sundown. We're nighthawks, remember?"

"Right."

Willo plunks her bill on my back and is soon snoring.

I slip out from under her cuddle. My eyes close to slits. I'm still buzzed from our death-defying flight through the mountains. I stare at the crashing waves, the fierce sun on the water, the mane of white spray flying down the beach.

My whole body jerks when I spot the silhouette of a big bird dropping from the sky. It swoops in and out of the spray. It levels off, flips on its back, and flies *upside down* over the cresting waves.

My eyes pop open and I crane my neck to watch it. *Whoa, nice move, Dude!*

The bird flies way down the beach until my view is blocked by a clump of palm trees. I shake my head wondering if I'm dreaming.

The waves, the sun, the spray. All there.

Not dreaming.

Squeerk!

I look up to where the weird sound came from. The same bird is already streaking down to the beach.

That bird's amazing! How'd it get back up there so fast?

This time it's sliding out of the sky tail-first.

That's impossible. Who is that?

I know all too soon.

The mystery bird does a double barrel-roll and lands in a stinging spray of sand right in front of us.

Willo jolts awake and screams.

"Who-hah, who-hah. ¿Que pasa, amigos?"

With our backs up against the bedrock cliff, we stand beak to beak with a big black raven.

14

GONZO
Panama beach

Willo freaks and tries to blast up the cliff face. *"Queek-queek! Queek-queek!"*

The raven leaps up and bats her down with a wing before she's off the beach, easy as swatting a fly. "Relax, cheeken-face. You're going nowhere fast."

I puff up my chest and step toward the raven. "Hey, go easy on my sister!"

The raven thrusts his fat beak in my face. He cocks one unblinking eye at me, then the other, inhaling deeply as if enjoying a good meal. His breath smells of death and decay.

My joints stiffen, ready to snap. My stomach heaves. *Don't,* I tell myself. *Don't throw up in his face.*

"Hmm," says the raven. "Your seester, ees it?" He leans over Willo with the same cocking motion.

He seems to be sniffing more than looking, listening more than inspecting. Like there's some mysterious way this raven perceives his world.

"We have you outnumbered, Mr. Raven!" Willo cries.

"*Who-hah-hah-hah.* You scare me to beets!"

I shoot a wing in front of Willo. "Don't touch her!"

The raven whips his gaze back to me, making hollow popping noises with his beak. A dim memory crashes into my brain. A mockingbird once told me that you never want to hear that sound coming from a raven. I can't recall why not and, right now, I don't want to.

The feathers on the raven's head spring up almost doubling its size. They're all fuzz and I wonder if this dreaded predator is a juvenile like me. Rising above the fuzz are two eye tufts that are pure white. *Bizarre.*

The raven's eyes, all frosty blue. Something definitely weird about them.

These are my last thoughts as the raven flings open his beak and lunges for my head.

"That was, uh, some pretty fancy flying!" I blurt as I get a close-up view of the raven's terrible pink throat.

The raven pulls back, beak popping. "So, you liked that, deed you?"

Charm him up. Make him a sky god. "That tail-first thing," I say, finding my breath. "Awesome! What do you call it?"

The raven stares at me. "You like to do treex, tasty bird?"

"Uh … it's Wisp, actually. And, yes, I do. I *live* for them!"

"Not for long, I'm afraid." Again, the raven cranks open his beak.

"So what do you call it?"

The raven's eyes narrow. "*Glug-glug, glug-glug.* Call what?"

"That totally amazing thing you did, sliding out of the sky on your back."

"Oh, that. *Culo primero.* How you say, bum first. It ees nothing."

"*¡Fantasico!*" exclaims Willo.

Willo gets it. Stroke his ego. I'd forgotten she knew some Spanish. Picked it up from her weird friend Peevo.

Mental note: Ask Willo to teach me the basics. I might have to ask directions in Spanish. If we live through this.

A wavy line of shadows sweeps across the beach. I cringe to the low *whuhh-whuhh-whuhh-whuhh-whuhh* of big wide wings.

Funny thing, so does the raven.

"*Krrr-ok, krrr-ok, krr-ok.* Eh, Gonzo!" shouts another raven circling above them.

I count a mob of ten ravens, all dangling something wiggly in their talons. "Those cheeken-hawks are too bony for your leettle beak. Eat these instead!"

One by one, each raven swoops low and, with incredible accuracy, drops its load more or less smack on Gonzo's head. He scrunches his shoulders with each bomb load— ten slimy, slippery, half-alive, disgusting-looking jellyfish. "*¡Buen provecho, Gonzo!*" yells the lead raven, who is huge and bristling with white feathers. "*Krrr-ok, krrr-ok.*"

And they're gone.

The raven trapping us seems smaller, a notch less scary. It lifts its tail and fires a jet of chalk-white guano onto the sand.

"So ... uh ... those your buddies?" I ask.

"None of your beesness, tasty bird," Gonzo says, puffing up his glossy throat feathers, some of which are white.

Charm him, charm him! "I bet they can't *fly* like you."

Gonzo closes his eyes and leans back on his dinosaur feet. "Nobody flies like me."

"You truly own the skies!"

Gonzo makes a deep croaking sound that bounces off the cliff wall. "You know, cheeken-hawk, you teekle my funny bone."

"Yes, hah-hah-hah. It's good to laugh. Uh … makes your lungs strong so you can fly better."

Gonzo leans over me, eyeball to hairy eyeball. "You know," he says slowly, "it ees deestasteful to eat something that makes you laugh. I might speet you out half-chewed."

"Yuck," Willo says, trying to sound cheerful. "Pureed nighthawk."

Gonzo pounces on her. "What do *you* know about deesgusting food, cheeken-face? Every day I have to go to the village, raiding dumpsters to eat human feelth. Rotten tomatoes, moldy doughnuts, slimy cheeken bones. I am seek of eating roadkeels and garbage." He gives Willo a long sniff. "What I love is fresh meat. The fresher the better."

"Uh … I know where you can get lots of that," I say "Easy pickings!"

Gonzo cocks a frosty eye at me. "Oh?"

I have no idea where I'm going with this. Anything to get the raven's mind off nighthawk meat. "Yeah, this place just crawling with caribou."

"Care-ee-boo. What ees that?"

"They're like … uh … deer. Only bigger."

"How am I supposed to keel that?"

"Oh, you don't have to. You just follow the wolves around and they do it for you. There's millions of them."

"Wolves?"

"Caribou."

"Meelions?"

"Yeah, all over the place."

"What place?"

"The Tundra."

Willo fires me a crazy look. "What are you—"

I ignore her. "You know, the land of the midnight sun."

"Meednight sun?"

"Yeah, the sun never sets. You find some wolves; follow them around; they take out a caribou; and *presto*, instant raven feast!"

At the sound of a distant raven call, Gonzo jerks his fuzzy head over his shoulder, scanning the sky in that weird way of his.

I glance at Willo for some kind of support. She gives me her *Are you out of your head?* eyes.

I shrug and wade deeper into trouble. "You'd love it there," I say to Gonzo.

A dying jellyfish tries to crawl up his leg. He flicks it onto the blazing sand. "How ees that?"

"All the fresh meat you could dream of. No bully ravens. No darkness to spoil your fun. Endless time and space to practice that amazingly awesome, fantastic flying you do."

Gonzo leans closer, suffocating me in dumpster breath. "I theenk you are making all thees up."

"No, honest. I—"

Another shadow sweeps across the beach, this one so big

it eclipses the sun. My stomach collapses. The three of us—yes, Gonzo, too—cower against the cliff.

My stomach unclenches at the sound of soft purring from a thousand throats.

An innocent flock of sandpipers.

They fall out of the sky in a living cloud, swerving, swooping, twisting, turning as one body. They slide down to the beach and land in the wet sand, skittering back and forth in time with the breaking surf.

It's begun! I think, forgetting even Gonzo for a moment. *The migration has really begun!* I know from stories I heard on the way south that shorebirds are the first spark in the explosion of spring migrators. The sight of so many birds, already massed and moving north, makes me frantic to be off to the Tundra.

If only I could ditch this crazy raven.

"*Krrr-ok, krrr-ok.*" Gonzo leaps backward onto the beach, trying to recover his ferocious bearing. "You have been to thees place?"

My throat dries up. "Oh, sure, lots of times."

Willo jabs a wing into my ribs.

"You know thee way?"

"Could do it with my eyes closed."

"Wisp!" hisses Willo.

"Then you weel take me there."

The bottom falls out of my stomach. "But ... uh ... well, I don't really—"

"If you don't find it," Gonzo says, casually stretching his wings into a terrifying black wall, "I can always eat you for a snack, tasty bird."

15

PLUMABLANCA
Panama beach

Shielded by his mighty squadron, Flare fears no flying thing. Well, except for bats. And ravens, of course. What nighthawk isn't afraid of ravens? When he spots a large mob of ravens loafing on the beach, it's all he can do to swallow the bile stuck in his throat.

Like it or not, he must talk to them. He must find out if they have seen Wisp.

The odds are good they have. Flare knows that almost every bird that flies north along the mountain flyway has to spill out somewhere along this particular beach.

"Dive!" he shouts. "Form a chain behind those ravens. Keep the ocean at your back. Don't take your eyes off those devils."

The ravens don't lift a feather as the diamond-shaped

flock swoops out of the sky and spreads across the wet sand behind them.

Flare looks them over, trying to figure out the mob's pecking order. The most important question: *Who's boss?* But he is foiled by the ravens' bizarre poses.

Flare clears his throat.

No response.

He coughs.

Nothing.

Then, without warning, the entire mob explodes into a cloud of glossy black feathers.

Flare's crack team of Guardians scatters like a swarm of startled moths.

"Cowards!" yells Flare who stands alone and defenseless on the beach. "Resume your positions!"

One by one, Flare's Guardians trickle back to the beach, each shadowed by a raven at its back. Flare curses under his breath for stopping here. He knows this could end badly for his squadron. Very badly.

"*Pok-a-pok-a-pok! Krrr-ok, krrr-ok, krrr-ok!*" shrieks the biggest raven who has parked himself behind Flare. "Hah! Scared you, goofy cheeken-hawks!"

"Uh … good afternoon, sir," Flare says with an odd squeak in his voice. He hopes he can handle this without Peevo's diplomatic grease. "Actually, we're not hawks but nighthawks. What you call *chotocabras.*" Flare thinks this sounds pretty impressive, a word he's been rehearsing all through the mountains. "And we come in peace."

"Big fat *chotocabras!*" says the raven behind him who keeps jumping out of view. "Soon to be in *pieces*, I theenk! ¿Eh, *amigos?* Juicy pieces!"

The other ravens make deep-throated gurgling sounds, which Flare takes for laughter. He feels his nape feathers twitch. His throat turns to dust.

Flare opens his beak but nothing comes out. He turns to Striker and angrily mouths two syllables at him.

"Sir?" says Striker.

Flare tries again, managing to whisper only the first syllable.

"Uh ... excuse me, sir. You have to go *pee*?"

"Pee-vo, you dolt!" Flare spits. "Get her!"

The raven behind Flare launches into the air and lands a beak-length from his eyes. He's a big brute, three times Flare's size, with a gigantic beak and a peculiar halo of bone-white feathers around his neck. "What ees the matter? You swallow a frog? Maybe we can feesh it out for you, no?"

More gurgling noises and the snapping of raven beaks.

"A leetle early for cheeken-hawks like you to be migrating, no? What ees the rush? Why don't you stay and make peekneek with us?"

This suggestion is met with a jolly chorus of "*Who-hah! Who-hah!*"

Peevo makes a perfect sideslip landing beside her Commander. "What's the problem, sir?"

"Tell him!" Flare barks in a hoarse whisper.

"Sir?"

"What we're doing!"

"Uh ... yes, sir." Peevo bows low before the raven boss who is more like four times her size. "Sir, we have come from the Amazon. This is my Commander, Flare, and I am Peevo, Chief Translator. We are a special squadron of nighthawks sent to—"

"*Mucho gusto*, midget goofy-hawk. I am *Plumablanca*, Chief Beach Bum."

Hysterical raven laughter all around him.

"Ah, yes," Peevo says calmly. "Plumablanca. White-feather. I have heard of your clan."

"You have?" both Flare and the raven burst out.

"Yes, indeed. I have heard how you were once the protectors of all birds funneling through this beach on the way to and from the mountains."

Plumablanca arches his back and looks up at the sky. "That sounds like horse feathers to me."

More beak snapping and lively thwacking of wings against the sand.

"So, what else do you know about us?"

Peevo hops closer to Plumablanca and looks up into his dark flashing eyes. "I have heard how your ancestors rose from a special line of white-headed ravens that descended from bald eagles."

"Hah! You mean those big, bossy feesh-eaters?"

"Exactly. *Fish*-eaters. Not bird-eaters."

"And not road-keel eaters, either, I theenk, or dumpster-divers."

More laughter.

"No, I think not, sir. With their stomachs full of fish, your ancestors gained god-like powers by protecting birds, not killing them."

"God-like! What are you talking, crazy goofy-hawk?"

"Oh, yes. Rivers of migrating birds passed through here, many more than today. Your ancestors chased away any predators roaming the beach—coyotes, owls, snakes, even early humans. The story goes that the gods granted your white-headed raven clan all the fish they could eat, so long as they protected other birds from these predators."

Plumablanca lifts his head and puffs out his feathers, revealing what looks like white eyebrows. All the other ravens hunch their shoulders and point their beaks to the sand. "How do you claim to know all thees, clever goofy-hawk?"

"I am the squadron's cultural expert. I know all the Amazonian languages. I talk. I listen."

"It ees a good story, no?" Plumablanca leans forward and smothers Peevo in his shadow. "But it sounds a leetle *feeshy* to me."

The other ravens make approving knocking sounds in their throats.

"Now, before we start peekneek, tell us, what ees *your* story?"

"Certainly, sir. Our migration does not actually begin for a few weeks. We are a special advance party searching for a vagrant nighthawk who has caused much trouble for our Colony."

"Oh, I see," says Plumablanca, "What kind of trouble?"

"He is wanted for rebelling against our Colony's laws. He migrates when and where he likes. We suspect he is now flying to a forbidden land where the sun never sets."

"Hmm. Very eenteresting."

"We have been sent to capture and punish this vagrant before his bad example spreads chaos through our Colony."

"Well, you weel find no chaos here, *señorita*. We are peace-loving ravens. Especially *juicy* pieces!"

"*Who-hah! Who-hah!*" goes the mob.

Peevo doesn't budge.

Flare goes green watching Peevo, so cool, beak-to-beak with this creepy predator.

"Have you seen any other nighthawks lately?" Peevo asks.

Plumablanca solemnly shakes his head. "Seen? No. Eaten? Maybe. We like to catch your kind at night. It ees more ... how you say ... sporting."

More *who-hahs*.

"What about Gonzo?" shouts another raven. "He was chewing on a couple."

"Gonzo?" wheezes Flare.

Plumablanca snaps his beak. "Just some loco raven."

Striker lets go a sigh. "Our search could be over, sir."

"Shut up."

Plumablanca rises to his full height, glaring at Flare. "*¿Perdon, Capitan?*"

Flare feels his throat closing. "Uh ... not you. Him."

Plumablanca's eyes clamp shut.

Flare detects a serious loss of mischief in Plumablanca's body language. The word part of Flare's brain shuts down. All he can do is stare dumbly at the raven.

Peevo to the rescue. "So, you saw two nighthawks?"

Plumablanca studies Peevo for a moment. "*Sí, señorita.* They were midgets like you but with white on their wings, not pretty gold like yours."

"And you believe, sir, that this Gonzo chap *ate* them?"

"Well, you know, he really prefers to eat steenky jellyfish."

Crazy gurgles and glugs.

"But I theenk he fly weeth them along the cleef."

"What direction?"

"North."

"When?"

"Yesterday." The raven boss flaps his wings. "Too many questions. *¡Vamos a comer!*"

All the ravens stomp on the Guardians' tails.

"What? What?" Flare croaks to Peevo.

"He said, 'Let's eat.'" Peevo holds her ground. "Please, sir, just one more question. Why would Gonzo migrate with nighthawks?"

"We don't migrate with anyone, anywhere," scoffs Plumablanca. "Gonzo ees crazy bird like the one you chase, no? Ruffles my feathers *mucho.*" He leans forward, looking hungrily at Flare. "Too bad we deed not eat all three of them while we had thee chance."

Enough talk, thinks Flare. Enough monkeys drooling over us. We can still catch Wisp. He gives Plumablanca a nervous nod and sets his wings for take-off.

Plumablanca erects a wall of feathers in front of him. "*Con permiso, Capitan*, but can you geev me one good reason why we not start peekneek now itself?"

Flare darts a glance at Peevo who goes still as a stone. She looks past her Commander, past her potential killer, out to the open ocean.

Flare knows that look. Peevo is thinking.

Not one of Flare's strong points.

All the ravens stop jumping about and watch her.

"I have it," Peevo says, turning to Plumablanca. "You're sorry you didn't eat those birds, even this Gonzo character?"

"Oh, yes, *señorita.* Sometimes we get tired of dumpster diving. And it will be many days before the migrators come to our beach for spring peekneek. Until we learn how to fish again, we will be forced to eat them."

Hilarious laughter.

"We can deliver these birds to you, sir."

"Even that lousy Gonzo?"

"We will take to him whatever message you want. Perhaps something suggesting that it's safe to return, that you won't bother him anymore. Then, when he comes back, you do what you like with him."

Plumablanca folds his wings over his back and stares down at Peevo. "I am not allergic to raven meat, or *chotocabra*."

Flare has regained a pinch of confidence and so, his voice. He shoves Peevo aside. "Sir, we have the skills, the strength, and the numbers to carry out this mission for you. Even if we have to track them across the continent, we will find them."

"Hmm. It ees true, we do not know much beyond the beach, the village." Plumablanca shrugs. "Why bother to make such beeg treeps?"

"Leave that to us, sir."

"You know, thees could be fun. Okay, you can go."

Flare lifts his wings. "Thank you, sir. We will—"

Plumablanca steps on Flare's feet. "But on one condeeshun. You leave someone with us."

"A hostage, sir?"

"Whatever. We trade when you come back weeth those three ... how you say ... *vagrants*."

Flare scans his squadron, slowly looking from Guardian to Guardian.

All avoid his gaze.

All but Peevo who steps forward. "I'll stay, sir."

As much as Flare depends on Peevo, he resents her

brains, her courage, and her speed. *Won't be vexed by her anymore.* "So be it. Catch you later, Peevo."

Pumablanca nods and all the ravens step back from their Guardian prisoners.

"Let's go, boys!" Flare shouts. *"Kill-ree! Kill-ree!"*

There is a great rush of wings and the squadron is off.

"¡El Capitan!" shouts Plumablanca from the beach. "My message to Gonzo. Tell him, 'We forgeev and forget. We mees you. Please come home soon!'"

Flare looks down to see a ring of ravens rolling every which way across the beach.

In the middle of them is a motionless nighthawk looking smaller than ever.

Striker assumes his regular flight position near the leading edge of Flare's diamond-shaped flock. "You trust those kooks to give her back?"

"They'll be dining on her before sundown."

"But—"

"It's Wisp I want. Captured. Punished. Dead. That's what I want."

16

OVER THE VOLCANO
Popocatépetl Volcano, Mexico

"Do you really have any clue where you're going, tasty bird?"

I've been dreading this question, wondering when Gonzo would get wind of my secret. That I'm a navigational zero. I'd managed to fake it north of Panama by clinging to the coast. A no-brainer. But I lost my grip somewhere over the mangrove swamps of Guatemala when stormy winds off the Pacific pitched us inland. Our Great Leader—me—has been wandering this way and that ever since.

"I do so know where we're going," I lie.

Luckily, Willo remembers a few major landmarks, like the mega-cone of Popocatépetl now looming before us. Amazingly, I missed this on the way south. Must've deked off the main flyway again to hang out with some roving stunt flier.

Already I can smell the rotten-egg stink from the volcano. I don't know if it's the fumes or the high altitude that Gonzo insists we fly at, but I'm feeling woozy way up here.

Praying that Gonzo won't notice, I tweak the angle of my wings and send us into a gradual descent into thicker air. Where I can breathe. Where my wings have more bite.

A wicked impulse strikes me. Slow down, make sure Gonzo's right on my tail, steer straight for the volcano's mouth, then pull up at the last moment. Oops! Gonzo gets boiled alive in bubbling lava.

Hmm, maybe not. Could lose Willo, too.

Instead, I adjust our flight path to go around Popocatépetl.

"All you do, Gonzo, is zip around this volcano, whiz through the desert, and soon you're cruising through the Rocky Mountains. Then skip over the prairies, make a dash for the Boreal Forest, wait for the trees to thin out, and, hooray, you're on the Tundra, stuffing yourself on fresh caribou."

I've gone over this route in my head a hundred times, pieced together from fuzzy memories of my zigzag flight south and the few crumbs I've managed to pick from Willo's brain.

It won't be that easy, of course. No nighthawk has ever made this journey—from the Amazon to the Arctic. If I don't die of starvation, get blown out to sea, shot by a human, eaten by a predator, or get back on Gonzo's menu, I just might make it to the Tundra.

I can do this. I can find a way. I don't need any dumb stars. I'm a survivor. I can find food anywhere. Make friends anywhere—as long as they're not nighthawks. I can find a way to ditch Gonzo. Willo, too, once we're far enough north and I don't need her help navigating. I can escape there. Alone and free.

My secret will be safe on the Tundra.

Then I remember Flare. He can't steal this prize from me. He can't.

"You make it sound so eesy, Weemp."

That's the whole idea, loopy raven. So easy that you ditch your trusty nighthawk guide and *vamos* on your own.

Happy trails, Gonzo.

Good riddance.

Two problems, though.

First, ravens don't migrate. Normal ravens, at least. One thing I know for sure, Gonzo is not normal.

Second, the farther we get from Gonzo's beachside turf, the more he leans on me to navigate. *What a joke that is.* And not just guiding him to the Tundra. Mr. Macho Raven can barely steer around basic stuff like trees, cliffs, and communication towers. What's worse, he tries to hide his need for my help by laying on the tough-guy talk.

"*¡Ay caramba!* What are you doing, Weemp?"

Uh-oh. He's on to my tweaks.

"Why do you keep fooling around with our flight-path?" he shouts. "We stay high. Got that? You are making me very peessed off! Very hungry for *chotocabra* meat!"

Willo zips to my side. "You're pissing him off again!" she whispers. "Talk nice. Humor him."

"I'm sick of babysitting this bully."

"*Krrr-ok, krrr-ok.* What are you wheespering about, cheeken-brains? You theenk I don't have ears?"

"Nothing, Gonzo. So ... uh ... you see that smoke up ahead? Kinda stinks and, well, you never know what a volcano this big will—"

Gonzo thrusts himself in front of me, flips on his back, and shoves his dinosaur feet at my head. "Of course, I can see it! What do you take me for, some kind of bat?"

"Bully off, Gonzo!" On impulse I turn his charge into a challenge. *Let the aerobatic contest begin!*

I flare my wings and plummet into a spiral dive. My ears sing to the rushing wind. My heart hums at full tilt. I tuck in one wing and spin like a dust-devil. I tuck in the other and drop like a stone.

No way that big lummox can keep up.

But he does.

I dart a glance backward and see him snapping for my tail even as he copies my every move. *How does he do that when he can barely fly around a tree?*

Snap-snap. I feel a stabbing pain in my rump.

"Ouch! Lay off!" I yell. I resume level flight, defeated by Gonzo's incredible flying prowess. "I never called you a bat. Jeez! What's the big deal?"

"The deal is thees, Weemp," he says, spitting out one of my tail feathers. "We go where *I* say!"

Something pops inside and fizzes over. "Yeah, but *you* haven't got a clue where you're going, you big black brute!"

As if I do.

"Oh yeah, cheeken-fart? You could not fly your way out of a paper bag."

"What would I know about paper bags, garbage-breath? I didn't grow up in a dumpster!"

Gonzo takes a swipe at my head with his massive wing.

Enough to knock my beak off if I hadn't ducked.

I barrel-roll out of the way and drop into a steeper dive. "Come on, Willo!" I shout, having no idea where she is. "Time to say *adios* to Fuzzhead. We're cutting loose!"

"*Quork-quork!*" Gonzo does a full wing-tuck and plummets straight for me. He catches up in seconds, casually flips on his back, and blocks my descent. "Not so fast, Weemp! Thees promised land you speak of, the Tundra, I do not believe you have even seen it."

"Have so!"

"I theenk you lie to me."

I flutter above Gonzo, jealous of how easily he flies upside down—even *hovers* upside down. "Okay, you're right. I made it all up. There's no such place. So let's just call the whole thing off. You go back to your dumpster and we'll—"

"I do *not* live in a dumpster, mouse-beak!"

"Okay, whatever. Go back to your beach so your buddies can kick sand in your face and drop crap on you."

Looking at Gonzo's flashing eyes, I realize it's not hunger I see. Not just plain old anger. It's a temper as hot as that volcano. And I think I just pushed him too far.

Best flier. Biggest temper.

I don't like where this is going.

"*Kek-kek-kek!*" shrieks Gonzo as he lunges for me, claws extended.

I duck out of range with a tidy flick-roll.

Gonzo gives chase, hurling a volley of *krrr-ok, krrr-ok* calls after me.

"Can't catch me, you sack of feathers!" I yell, pulling up into a vertical climb.

Gonzo gains on me but, just before he can clamp his fat

beak on my tail, I drop into a sidewise wingover and scream past him in the opposite direction.

Gonzo follows in hot pursuit.

I try to lose him in the thickening steam.

Snap-snap.

I can't afford to lose any more tail feathers. Time for evasive action. I suddenly pull into an inside loop. The force on my body wants to tear out my breastbone and spill my guts into the sky.

Again, Gonzo echoes every flap, every turn.

But he can't catch me.

Just as I'm about to start the upswing part of the loop, I stop flapping. Gonzo shoots past me as I fall backward tail-first. I slip into a stall, then nosedive into a graceful outside loop.

A scissor-tailed flycatcher taught me that trick. Called it the tail-slide loop.

Hah! Lost him!

I'm used to practicing aerobatics alone. But I have to admit that, even though Gonzo could rip me apart with a flick of his beak, having him on my tail adds to the fun. Actually, the most fun I've had, *ever.*

Then it hits me.

When it comes to speed, I've got Gonzo beat. His wide wings are no match for my feathered daggers.

"Hey!" I yell as I watch Gonzo struggle to regain altitude. *"¿Que pasa, amigo?"*

"Very funny, *loco* cheeken!"

I can't help laughing at my supposed captor until I realize I have no idea where my sister is.

A familiar feeling on this trip.

"Willo! *Queek-queek! Queek-queek!*"

"Up here, goof!" comes a voice from high above. "Will you, like, wait up?"

She zigzags down to me, her flight still choppy from her bashed tail feathers.

Gonzo labors up to us, buffeted by a new air turbulence from the volcano.

Before any bird can say anything, the volcano speaks, emitting a long, earth-shaking rumble.

"*¡Perfecto!*" exclaims Gonzo, who seems to have cooled off after a dose of stunt flying. Or maybe my victory earned me a trace of respect. Whatever. At least he's not talking about *chotocabra* meat.

I stop in mid-flap and hover. "What do you mean?"

"I mean we're in for a beet of fun, cheeken-wings. You said you live for treex?"

"Well, yeah, but—"

"Then what for go around thees volcano? A beeg waste of hot air. We weel go over it, *comprende*, Weemp?"

I turn to Willo and shrug. She keeps surprising me with her Spanish.

"He's saying, 'Get it, Wimp?'"

"Now don't *you* start calling me that."

I pump my wings to catch up to the bird I was fleeing moments ago. "Uh ... sure, Gonzo. But all that smoke. That rumbling. Don't you think it might be better if we—"

"Notheeng to worry about. I tell you, nowhere weel you find better thermals. There ees one of these not far from my beach that I like to play in. Over volcanoes, the thermals they are ... how you say ... *awesome!*"

I know all about playing in thermals. A turkey vulture

once showed me how to find them along the edge of the Grand Canyon. But after a few near-crashes into the canyon walls, I decided that I sucked at it.

"I'm game ... I guess."

"Are you nuts, Wisp?" Willo says. "Look at that thing!"

I have to admit the volcano's plume has gotten scarier since the rumbling started. But in a weird kind of way, I trust Gonzo to get us in and out of the thermals without frying our butts. "Like you said, humor him."

"*¡Vamos! ¡Vamos!*" croaks Gonzo, headed straight for a city due east of us.

Where in the world is he going? "Uh ... hey, Gonzo, the volcano's *this* way!"

Gonzo wheels around. His frosty eyes leak a hint of embarrassment, a flicker of fear.

I know that look. Like me, he's hiding something. What?

"Of course, cheeken-guts! I am just ... uh ... checking the wind direction."

"Right."

Instead of banking low around Popocatépetl, I lead us straight across its belching cone. We rise five thousand wingbeats above the plume. Even way up here, the heat and sulfur sting my eyes. Explosive pops and gurgling sounds waft up to us from the red-hot lava lake that fills the crater.

Gonzo is in heaven, with eyes closed, drunk on a thermal high.

Willo and I watch as he spirals up and up on unflapping wings.

"Try eet. You'll like eet!" Gonzo shouts down to us. "Just trust your weengs! Don't feedle with them! Shut up your brain!"

In just one year, I've probably had more flight instructors than most nighthawks have in a lifetime. Snow geese, vultures, golden plovers, arctic terns, and that fly-catcher who taught me the tail-slide loop. *But a raven?* A raven who tried to eat me—and might yet?

Now I know I can outfly him on a breakneck dive. As long as I humor Gonzo like Willo says, help keep his belly topped up, and watch my back, I might actually learn something from him.

I've never met a fancier flier.

I watch with open beak as the thermals lift Gonzo almost out of sight.

"We're getting out of here," Willo announces.

"What?"

"He'll never catch us now."

She's right—as usual. We could dive into the steam and be out the other side before Gonzo even opens his eyes. It's a good plan. It makes total sense. What sane nighthawk would do otherwise?

Ditch Gonzo or throw myself at his dinosaur feet to learn more flying tricks. I clench my beak. The choice is obvious. "Might as well try it while we're here, eh?"

"Are you nuts?"

"It's not every day you get to play in thermals like this."

"Gonzo's loony! He almost bit your head off at that beach."

My rump still stings where he plucked out a feather. But I've made up my mind. "He's not so tough. You saw how he freaked when those other ravens teased him."

Willo spins tight circles around me. "Nighthawks just don't do that!"

"Do what?"

"Like, *soar.*"

"Says who? Come on, try it."

"No way."

Willo's got it wrong this time. I shoot out my wings.

The air shreds beneath me and I tumble sideways toward the lava lake, feeling ridiculous.

"See?" Willo yells.

"*Who-hah! Who-hah!*" Gonzo croaks from way, way up.

I drop into an uncontrolled dive until I taste sulfur at the back of my throat. I let myself fall farther into the fumes, ready to puke. I so hate failing at anything. I so hate when Willo's right. *Nighthawks just don't do that.*

Then I remember Gonzo's last instruction: *Shut up your brain!*

I flare my wings, braking just a few hundred wingbeats from the volcano's belching mouth. I claw my way up through the steamy air until I'm in the clear.

Flap flap flap ... glide. Flap ... glide. Flap flap ... glide. That's how all nighthawks do it, right? That's how they fly.

Not me.

I'm ready for something different. I extend my wings, this time flexing them slightly. I hold them taut and still.

For a nighthawk, not flapping is like holding your breath. After a while, you feel like you're going to explode. You can't fight it.

But I fight this. I fight the urge to flap.

My whole body fights back.

At first it's like my wings will snap off. My flight muscles scream for some action. Fire fills my veins. I'm about to grind my beak into splinters.

Everything feels so wrong. This is stupid.

Shut up your brain!

Okay, Gonzo. For once, I'll play your game.

I let go. I close my eyes and surrender to the hot rising air. Gravity dissolves.

A powerful beam seems to drop from the sky, magically drawing me higher and higher into the air. The normal whistle of wind through my wings fades to a whisper, a sigh, then ... nothing. I can hear hissing and rumbling from the volcano now far below. From way above comes a gurgly "*Quork-quork!*" An approving grunt from Gonzo?

I don't care if he's watching. I don't care if Willo's watching. Anything I once called "me" shrinks and disappears. All I am is a fleck of ash, a leaf, a flower petal, floating in the thermals.

I soar, actually soar.

Weightless.

Without a flap.

Without a thought.

Without effort.

I've never felt so free.

"Wisp!"

Guess who.

"Wisp!" Willo yells. "Nighthawks! A whole bunch of them."

I open my eyes and follow Willo's anxious gaze to a diamond-shaped flock sweeping over Popocatépetl's ash-smeared shoulder.

17

DETOUR
Puebla, Mexico

"Gonzo's right," Willo whines as we flee from Flare and his thugs. "You don't have a clue where you're going!"

Tell me something I don't know. "I do so. Just follow me, okay?"

"Yeah, but—"

"You want Flare as a traveling buddy?"

That shuts her up. But she's on to my secret. I'll have to try harder to fake it. Won't ask her any more directions. Do my best to navigate by the sun, by crosswinds—I don't know, maybe even by odors. No kidding. A blue jay told me he could do it. Hah, there's a plan. I'll *smell* my way to the Tundra. I'll try anything as long as I don't have to depend on anyone else.

Especially Willo. What if she found out what's really wrong with me? What if Flare catches us and drags us back to the Refugium? She'd eventually blab. Then I'd be as good as dead. Worse than dead.

A Plebeian nighthawk who can't read the stars. What good is that?

Nothing.

Son of a fully initiated Navigator, yet?

Less than nothing.

It's no surprise Willo wonders what I'm up to. We fly north, north, north, day after day. Then I hang a sharp right and lead us due *east*? I had to do it. After spotting Flare's squadron over Popocatépetl, I decided to bolt anywhere but north.

I'd noticed this city when Gonzo took off in the wrong direction. Puebla. That's what Willo called it. It really bugs me how she knows all this stuff. Since we left Ecuador, she's been able to name just about every big landmark and town along the way. Willo likes to organize the world into safe, orderly pieces. Likes to follow the rules. She devours names and numbers. Mom must've fed her a pile on their way south. They're a lot alike that way.

Me? That kind of stuff goes in one ear and out the other.

Anyway, I chose this direction because I know Guardians don't care much for humans. Scared of them, actually. Bats, ravens, and humans. That's why Dad picked a school roof to nest on. He knew they'd never bother us there. And they won't bother us in Puebla, either. Even if Flare does somehow trail us here, I've buzzed over enough cities to know there'll be lots of places to hide.

Gonzo's not exactly thrilled with my route change. He

soared so high on those thermals, I thought we'd seen the last of him. But the instant I swung east, he came bombing out of the sky and started screaming at me about what a *loco* navigator I am.

Good call, Gonzo.

Crazy Gonzo. Something about him doesn't make sense. He can barely dodge a telephone pole, yet he can track our flight path from ten thousand wingbeats above us. Or chase my tail, copying every stunt I make.

Luckily, there's a big dump at the edge of town and I zoom straight for it. That'll keep him off me for a while.

For its size, Puebla's air is pretty clean. Its spires and domes are a lot less scary than the huge office towers I almost smacked into in other cities when I flew south. But a dump's a dump and this side of town is no bird park.

Thousands of shrieking seagulls wheel above the dump while thousands more peck away at its stinking surface. The rest of them peck each other. A few ragged-looking humans fling slimy bags into the air as they look for choice goodies. There's lots to go around and Gonzo dives right in.

Willo and I perch on one of the railway tracks that hug this side of the dump. The gravel and dog crap lining the tracks sparkle with broken glass.

"What now?" Willo asks.

"We wait."

"For what?"

"For when I feel okay about heading north again."

"Flare could never find us."

"Here? No." I point one wing to what I guess is north. "Out there? I don't know. I just don't get how he tracks us." I instantly regret saying this. *How's that for inspiring confidence in your fearless leader?*

"I'm hungry."

Me too. Starved. All that stunt flying over the volcano took a lot out of me.

I can find bugs in just about any kind of wild country that North or South America can throw at me. But hunting in a city? Not one of my specialties.

"I said, I'm hungry."

"Yeah, I got you the first—"

We both turn our heads to the sound of bouncing rocks. A scrawny boy dressed in rags is throwing gravel at a rusty streetlight dangling over the track. I notice that both his feet are a spider's web of scars, probably from walking over all the glass.

Hmm. Streetlight. "I got it," I say. "When it gets dark, there'll be tons of bugs buzzing around that light."

"Can't wait that long."

The boy starts inching toward us, several rocks in hand. I may not be able to read stars but I can read that look on his face. Hunger. It hits me that we're not at all camouflaged against the shiny tracks.

"Fly!" I shout, turning to Willo. But she's already gone, smacked sideways by a whizzing rock.

I hover above Willo's crumpled form, hurling shrill *"Queek-queek! Queek-queek!"* alarm calls at the boy. He advances. I dive bomb him, again and again, aiming for his head. He holds up one hand while bending over for more rocks with the other. He fires one at me and clips my right wing. The impact sends me tumbling through the air and I bounce off one of the tin shacks beside the tracks.

When I look again, the boy is running for Willo who's still sprawled on the ground. He's holding a big flat rock in both hands. Willo flaps wildly, sending a spray of broken glass and dog crap into his face.

I strafe the boy again. He's almost on her, raising the flat rock above his head, when Willo makes a lopsided lift-off and zips right between his legs.

I swoop to her side, ignoring the stinging pain at the tip of my wing. I'm shocked to see how slow Willo's flight is, choppier than ever. Pathetic. In her condition, she'd never outfly a Guardian.

But she's airborne and out of range of flying rocks. I hear the boy spouting Spanish words that need no translation. "No *chotocabra* meal for you, kid!" I shout back, which, to him, probably sounds like irritated squeaks.

With lots of coaxing, Willo's able to climb high above the city. We're both shaken up but, the instant we level off, we break into a fit of nervous laughter, just happy to be alive and able to fly, however sloppily.

I don't have a clue where Gonzo is and at this point I couldn't care less. That skizo raven, thrilling me with his "*treex*" one moment, thrusting his claws at me the next. I just don't have the energy right now to figure him out. Something tells me that if he really wants to find us, he will.

I tip my wing, ready to turn my back on Puebla, when I spot a large banana-shaped pond right beside the dump. I can't imagine how gross the water is in that pond, but I guess from all the plants growing on it that it must be loaded with bugs.

"Still hungry?" I ask.

"I'd even go for a fire ant right now."

"Let's check out that pond."

As we zoom toward it, I see that much of the water surface is covered with purple hyacinth blossoms, a prime breeding area for mosquitoes. "All right!" I say. And then, even better, I hear the lisping clatter of dragonfly wings.

In spite of her damaged wing, Willo goes for it, hunting back and forth over the pond. I'm about to join her when I see something zooming for her from the other side of the pond. In the glare of sun off the water I can't make it out. Some kind of fruit bat?

What I hear next freezes my wings.

Staccato flaps.

Too late to hide!

All I can make out is the bird's silhouette, showing the bulky profile of a Guardian nighthawk.

18

TRAPPED
Puebla, Mexico

"*Queek-queek! Queek-queek!*"

At the sound of Willo's alarm call, I know she's spotted the lone Guardian. I can't tell if he's spotted me. He seems intent on hunting Willo, following her every move with deadly accuracy.

I hover for a moment, gripped by a tempting plan that slinks into my mind. Beat it while I can. Ditch both Gonzo *and* Willo. My solo adventure to the Tundra will be back on track. My secret will be safe. Isn't Willo the one who wanted to return to the Refugium? And Gonzo? Why would he want to leave a classy dump like this?

I give my head a shake. *What am I thinking? Forget the Refugium. That Guardian might have orders to kill us on sight.*

There's only one way to save her.

"Come and get me, you big brute!" I yell. I swoop in front of the Guardian to lure him off Willo's tail. My plan is to get him to pursue me, then bolt for the jumble of shacks along the tracks where it should be easy to hide.

I fly out in the open, purposely slowing down to almost a stall so he can catch up. When I look back, he's still chasing Willo and closing fast.

Time for Plan B.

I zoom in front of Willo and steer her straight for the dump. "Follow me!" My hope is that we can lose ourselves inside the cloud of seagulls swirling over the dump. The Guardian will get all confused and we'll zip out the other side for the safety of the hills. I aim for a squawking clump of seagulls and dive right in. After just a few wingbeats, we lose our pursuer in a blur of white feathers.

Good plan.

Except I forget one important detail. Some birds, like, let's say seagulls, often mistake nighthawks for falcons or hawks and freak out whenever they see us.

The shit starts flying the moment the seagulls realize who's joined their flock—or who they *think* has joined them. That's their first line of defense. Poop on you. Then they start pecking.

If you've ever been attacked by an angry seagull, you know how sharp their big yellow beaks can be. I once saw two seagulls fighting over a pile of fish guts. The fight ended badly for the loser whose head was ripped off. That's how I feel when the rain of blows begins.

What a way to die!

Plan C pops into my head, or what's left of it.

"We're only nighthawks!" I shout. "Go for that falcon behind us!" The Guardian is way bigger. They just might believe me.

But the seagulls can't hear me above their own shrieking. The pooping and pecking only get worse. I find myself wishing they'd get it over with fast.

I close my eyes, bracing myself for a crash landing, when I realize that most of the shrieking is now behind me. Maybe they *did* hear me and are pecking the crap out of that Guardian.

I flick what poop I can off my wings and scan the sea of slime below me. I spot something fluttering on top of an overturned shopping cart.

Willo.

"You okay?" I shout as I streak toward her. "Willo?"

Before she can answer, I see the Guardian pop out of the seagull cloud. He's pumping straight for Willo and looking totally unruffled. I'm startled by what looks like *white* wingbars—not gilded—when I realize that he too has just emerged from a storm of gull poop.

"Get up! Get up!" I yell. "Willo!"

Her feeble tremors turn into flapping and she's up and away, though just barely.

"No ... wait, stop!" shouts the Guardian in a scratchy voice.

As if. My days of doing a Guardian's bidding are long gone, Buddy.

Again I take aim at the shacks along the rail line, hoping for a place to hide. With my body pecked half to pieces, my speed advantage is shot. I hardly recognize Willo, now covered in poop, slime, and blood. She flops through the air beside me, just a wingbeat away from disaster.

"Keep flapping!" I yell. "Don't give up!"

Where's Gonzo when you need him? He could take out this evil nighthawk in one fell swoop.

Probably up to his neck in rotting rats.

Did I just think that—*need* him?

"Please, stop!"

Please? It's the Guardian again. A voice I don't recognize. Not Flare, at least.

Just another hundred wingbeats or so and we'll be back over the tracks and can duck into the shadows.

A scary rumble seems to fall out of the sky. It soon gets the tin roofs rattling all around us. As we swoop down toward row after row of tracks, I see gravel dancing on the rail bed.

Is Popocatépetl about to pop?

"Wisp, look out!" Willo shouts.

A red locomotive appears around a sharp bend and comes barreling down the tracks.

With no time or strength to climb we dash across the tracks just as the locomotive clips past. The wind from its passage almost sucks us under the wheels.

With the Guardian so close on our tails, I'm crossing my feathers that he'll smack into the train before he can pull up. I look back and my beak drops when I see him scoot *under* the speeding rail cars like he's cruising through a marsh of swaying cattails.

Before I can even think of hiding, he chases us into a big cement culvert blocked at the other end with a screen of barbed wire.

19

TAMAS
Puebla, Mexico

I never knew we could get so fat. Most Plebeians are starving most of the time. At least the ones that choose to stay in the Refugium. Okay, the ones that aren't smart enough to escape like me, imprisoned there by Guardian goons.

But this is no Guardian.

I'd been right about his wingbars. They're white, not gilded. And no slashing claws or razor beak, either.

He's just a fat old Plebe.

"I'm so sorry I scared you," he says in that scratchy voice that no longer terrifies me. "It's just that I don't get many visitors, especially," he says, staring oddly at Willo, "ones so pretty."

"You sure seem at home with trains," I say, trying to get

his puffy eyes off my sister.

"Oh, yes, this *is* my home. I like to roost on the railway ties. It's good fun when the trains roll right over top of you. At least, it used to be. I hardly notice them anymore."

"So, like, how long have you lived here?"

"Oh, forever."

"Alone?" I ask.

"Yes. Not by choice, mind you. But everyone else seems determined to kill themselves migrating."

Good point. Here I am, barely into North America, and I've already been almost stung, burned, frozen, bitten, or pecked to death. "You don't migrate?"

"Why put myself through all that misery when I have everything I need right here?" He's looking funny at Willo again. "Well, *almost* everything."

"What do you mean?" I ask.

Another train rumbles by just a few wingbeats from our culvert. The old nighthawk doesn't even blink.

"You saw that pond," he continues, like nothing happened. "It's a virtual volcano of mosquitoes and dragonflies. Keeps me fat and happy."

I'll say. Fat, at least.

"And no predators. Between these trains and my friends the seagulls, I'm protected for life."

That's when I notice that, unlike Willo and me, all his feathers are intact. Not a speck of blood. Except for a few bomb-loads of poop, those seagulls didn't touch him.

"What about little boys with big rocks?" I ask.

"Oh, I get along fine with the local humans. One family along the tracks has sort of adopted me. Chases the rowdy kids away. Even leaves me a bowl of dead flies now and then."

Weird. Living alone. Mixing with other species like seagulls, even humans. But then that's what other nighthawks say about me. I realize we're not that different.

"Are you ... Tamas?" Willo asks.

There goes Willo with her names and numbers thing.

"Indeed, I am. How very clever of you."

Willo stares at him in disbelief. "But I thought you—"

"So does every vagrant nighthawk that occasionally passes through here. Got ripped apart by a jaguar, swallowed by a snake, plucked clean by howler monkeys. That's what Arwen says about everyone who escapes. Arwen, the queen of lies."

Now that's my kind of thinking. As peculiar as this nighthawk looks—it's a wonder he can fly really—there's something likeable about him. "You forgot sucked dry by vampire bats," I say.

Tamas snorts. "Just another fabrication to keep us under her beak. To make us believe there's no life beyond the Refugium and blind loyalty to her laws."

"You mean the Three Noble Oaths?" Willo asks.

"Ugh. Don't remind me," Tamas says. "Every vagrant who breaks free from all that steals a straw from Arwen's cushy nest. Snub the Oaths and you rob the Royals of their power. If one Plebeian can fly the coop unharmed, what's to stop others from doing the same? What's to stop a full-blown Plebeian rebellion? So, of course, Arwen has to execute us with her lies. To her, all vagrants are dead meat."

I recall the ripples of discontent I sensed just before I busted out. My fellow Plebes reciting the Three Oaths through clenched beaks. "Arwen will croak when she finds out we made it to the Tundra."

"My goodness," Tamas says. "Now there's a daunting destination. Forbidden territory."

"Third Oath," I say. *The one I hate most.*

"Oh yes," Tamas says in a pompous Arwen-like voice. "Blessed be the Boreal Forest, our one true summer home, beyond which there can be no life or liberty." He shakes his head in disgust. "It's a pity I still remember that."

"Why is the Tundra forbidden?" Willo asks.

"The official Royal line is that our stories stop at the Boreal. Beyond that, it's impossible to navigate. Arwen's supposedly protecting us from getting lost and dying a horrible death in the Arctic wastes. Yet another one of her ploys to fence us in."

My thoughts jump to my father. Why didn't he tell me this—*impossible to navigate*? To protect me from a lie? Or did he believe it himself? Did he really go to the Tundra or was he just telling more stories like Willo says? What about the giant raven story? Did he make that up, too?

Whatever, I'm going.

"I've been dreaming of the Tundra since before I could fly," I say, sounding much more confident than I feel.

"Ah … dreams," Tamas says wistfully. "I used to have such dreams." He lets go a sigh that echoes through the culvert. "A mountainside roost in Alaska. But all I found along the way were trials and trouble, distress and despair. This is as far as I got."

My deep-seated itch flares up at his words. "How can you *not* migrate? I mean, don't you ever get restless?"

"Oh, I didn't invent the idea."

"Other vagrants, you mean?"

"A clawful, perhaps. Most end up dead, I imagine. No, I'm talking about a Colony loyalist. A Guardian, in fact."

I pray it isn't him. "Who?"

"Flare. Creepy even for a Guardian. One of the main reasons I took off."

Can I relate!

"He has a plan to avoid *all* perils of migration by doing away with the whole nasty business."

"You mean … the *whole Colony* would not migrate?"

"Yes. And I dare say there's some merit in his plan. If he can convince Arwen, or, more likely, knock her off her Royal stump, he just might pull it off. Could save a lot of lives, except …" Tamas trails off as if maybe he's said too much.

All year in the Refugium? That's death, not life. "Except what?"

"Except, of course, if Flare succeeds in putting a stop to migration, then they won't need us anymore, will they? Who needs Plebeian Navigators when there's no place to go? Besides spotting the odd snake, we'd just be a drain on their food."

I'm not hearing this. "So …?"

Tamas squeezes his wings tight against his back. "I believe the correct term is … Plebeicide."

I've barely given my mother a thought since busting out. Just glad to be out of her feathers, mostly. I've gradually buried the thought that my escape got her into trouble. Denial can work wonders.

But now this. Flare's plan to end migration and wipe us out. Would he do it? Could a rebellion stop him? What would happen to Mom? How soon might all this begin—if it hasn't already? I guess the only bright side is that, as long as Flare is chasing us, he can't hatch his plan. Then again, catching and punishing us will only give him more proof that Plebes are more trouble than they're worth.

"That monster's after us right now!" Willo cries.

Tamas glances over his shoulder into the sweltering rail yard, "He is?"

"We ditched him at the volcano," I say, too matter-of-factly.

Tamas relaxes and hops closer to Willo, eyeing her up and down in a way I don't like. "There, there, pretty one. You'll be safe here with me. Flare's right, you know. Migration can get very messy. But wouldn't you rather stop it on your terms, not his? Like I say, I'm doing just fine here. Except I must admit I *do* get a little restless for company every springtime."

He wants to mate with her!

I'm feeling suddenly claustrophobic. In the gloom of the culvert and stink of the dump, I'd forgotten that we're plastered in seagull crap. "Uh ... look, Tamas, is there some place we could take a bird bath?" I launch into the air, my body pockmarked with pain.

"Yes, of course. The pond."

Eew! Bathwater supplied fresh from the dump. But I'm ready for any excuse to leave this horny old vagrant.

Willo struggles to catch some air.

"Please, let me escort you," Tamas says in an overly friendly way.

"No, really, that's okay," I say as a cloud of dread creeps over me.

"*Please*, I insist." And he's back on Willo, chasing her tail.

Weak as we are, Tamas could easily overpower us both to get what he wants.

Willo flops randomly through the air. It's all I can do to lead her around and around the rail yard, trying frantically to climb above the shacks.

Tamas is in hot pursuit, blind to all but Willo's barred and buffy breast.

He probably never even saw the train that took him out.

We'd just managed to rise high enough above the tracks when a lone locomotive came roaring down on him. It must have been a direct hit, judging by the explosion of feathers.

"That poor old bird really had the hots for you," I say as we rise above a dome-topped hill on the outskirts of Puebla. I'd spotted a little goldfish pond behind one of the churches and we're both feeling much better after a good bath. I doubt if the goldfish are.

"I'm not surprised he was lonely," Willo says, sounding awfully forgiving of Tamas's lusty advances. "He probably would've been a lot happier if he'd stayed with the Colony."

"Humph," I say, pouring on speed in spite of my bruised and weary muscles.

His real problem? He threw his dream away.

I point us north, at least, to what I *feel* is north. That's all I have to go on, a feeling. Rising from somewhere near the front of my skull. This feeling has been creeping up on me, like a morning breeze. Light as a feather. It's new, it's hazy, but I like to think it's real. Anyway, I know Willo will tell me if I'm screwing up again. *At least I won't have to listen to—*

"Hey, Weemp! Where do you theenk you are going?"

I'm stunned by the part of me that's glad to hear Gonzo's

voice. Then I think, *Who's more skizo here? Him or me?*

After Gonzo's usual tough-guy talk, and my usual pack of lies about what a great navigator I am, we both cool off and start trading stories about our Puebla adventures. I tell him about the scary kid with the rocks and the tragic tale of Tamas.

"*Who-hah!* What a waste of *chotocabra* meat!" Gonzo says. Then he boasts of finding untold riches in the dump and a female raven that he invited to the Tundra. "When I asked her, she just laughed een my beak!" He roars. "I knew that *señorita* was not thee one for me."

Seems there's love in the air these days.

Bah! What better way to throw away my dream.

Then again, it might be just the answer for my Gonzo woes. Maybe he'll find some sweetie along the way who'll tie him down. He'll return to his own kind. Start a flock of little *Gonzoitos*.

I know Gonzo's belly must be full to bursting, so I have nothing to fear from him for a while. We click back into our long-haul flight formation, me, Gonzo, then Willo. She took the worst of the stones and the pecks and now trails farther behind than ever. I'm praying she can hold it together until Yellowknife. I can safely dump her there, then finally, *finally*, push on to the Tundra.

Alone.

20

MAGGOTS
Sonoran Desert, Arizona

Flare now seems more threatening to me than ever. After spotting his squadron over Popocatépetl, I'd decided that we had no choice but to fly low to the ground, like bats. The usual kick I get from steady, rhythmic flight is wrecked by new questions jangling in my head. Is Flare ahead of us or behind us? Has he set up an ambush? Exactly who is chasing who here anyway? What are his orders if he captures us?

Then there's the question that's been niggling me ever since leaving Ecuador. Would those goons even be on my tail if Willo hadn't led them to me? Whatever. The fact is I'm a fugitive now, dashing for my life. Under the circumstances, flying low and fast seems like the best way to go.

Great idea if you're trying to avoid being captured or killed by Flare and his heavies.

Lousy idea if you're leading a blind raven across a continent.

That's right, blind.

"Pull up, Gonzo," I shout. "Another cactus!"

I had suspected something was weird with this raven from the moment I stood eyeball to eyeball with him on that Panama beach. Gonzo's secret finally came out one wet, windy night in Mexico's Sierra Mountains. We'd taken shelter in a cave while sitting out a monster lightning storm.

Gonzo's stomach was grumbling and, once again, he was looking at me funny.

I so hate when he does that. Nearly chokes me.

What saved my skin that time was an angry squeak from the back of the cave. "Heh-heh, Gonzo. Check it out," I said, finding my breath again.

Gonzo hopped into the darkness, there was a brief scuffle, and back he came with a fat kangaroo rat squished in his beak.

With his stomach happy for the moment, Gonzo got talkative, telling stories of his aerobatic feats back in Panama. He told how he'd been flying far out to sea, practicing his latest "treex," when a wicked wall of thunderclouds overtook him. He was sucked deep into the clouds. Locked in the storm, he made the best of it, enjoying the lightshow, surfing the choppy winds, until—*BOOM!*—a crackling flash of fire knocked Gonzo out of the sky.

He smacked into the sea and woke to a blank screen behind his eyes—which has lasted ever since. "Lucky my head was not blown to beets!" he'd said.

Something in me shuddered when the story of his blindness sank in. When I realized how easily he had shared his secret.

Maybe I'd misread him. Maybe it wasn't a big deal after all.

All I know is I could never expose my secret like Gonzo did.

Never.

Since that stormy night on the mountain, we'd agreed that Gonzo would tuck in tighter behind me, a plan I'm not exactly thrilled with. How would you like to have a rascally raven breathing down your back all day? But it means Gonzo is less likely to crash into stuff and I can concentrate on watching for Flare.

"Aw, Wisp!" That whine again. "We should be in the Rocky Mountains by now. We're totally off course!"

"Like, that's the whole idea, Willo. Stay off the beaten flyways. Flare would never look for us way out here."

"Yeah, especially if we turn to dust. I'm thirsty, Wisp. I'm hungry!"

I can barely swallow. My throat feels like it's lined with cactus needles.

I scan the bone-dry desert. Sun-baked boulders, straggly cacti, and half-dead scrub. It looks like it hasn't rained here for about a hundred years.

"So where are the careeboo?" Gonzo says.

I look over my shoulder at Gonzo, thinking maybe he's got sunstroke.

Then I get it. No trees.

From all the dumb questions Gonzo asks, I figure he knows diddly-squat about anything beyond his beach.

Since going blind, his world must have got even smaller. No surprise that Gonzo mistakes the Sonoran desert for Arctic Tundra.

"Uh ... we're not quite there yet, Gonzo." *Like, only a few million more wingbeats.*

"*Krr-ok, krr-ok!* Weemp, you are making my tail feathers steef. Do not play games with me, especially on an empty stomach!"

I see Gonzo lift his fat beak for a long sniff. On a good day, when Gonzo is well fed and we're making decent progress north, I can almost forget that look in his eye when I'm back on his menu.

This is not a good day.

Besides helping him find food—his kind of food—my only other safety net is to keep myself useful as his personal navigator, which is pretty funny. I sometimes get the feeling he really does ache for the Tundra, almost as much as I do.

One thing I am sure of. Gonzo senses a lot more than he lets on.

How, for instance, does he know there are no trees here? That night on the mountain, chewing on a kangaroo rat, he explained how, after he lost his sight, a new kind of vision gradually took its place. He started noticing swirly pink shapes dancing on the screen behind his eyes. It turned out these were lizards, birds, grasshoppers, humans—basically, anything with a heartbeat—all giving off a kind of liquid light that Gonzo can detect. He says the glow from plants is a lot tougher to make out but claims that, if he really concentrates, he can sense that, too. Even water, sometimes. He calls it *luz de vida*, the light of life.

Bizarre.

Beyond the glowy stuff, Gonzo is blind as a bat.

But his sense of smell is nothing to sneeze at. "There ees a fresh keel somewhere up ahead."

Thank the winds. That'll take his mind off nighthawk meat.

As usual, I can't smell a thing. "You smell it, Willo?"

"Pee-ew! Of course. But what good are dead animals to us? Give me a nice fat dragonfly or a—"

"Shh! It's for him. Keep him happy, remember?"

Willo falls into a sulky silence.

"Uh ... why don't you take the lead for once, Gonzo?" I say. "Follow your beak. We'll shout out if you're going to crash into anything."

Gonzo zooms past me with a great *whuhh-whuhh-whuhh-whuhh-whuhh.*

That sound still gives me the willies.

Gonzo leads us to a razor-sharp cliff that falls away into a narrow sandstone canyon. A ribbon of bright green cottonwood trees lines the canyon floor. We plunge into the canyon with Gonzo far ahead, his beak raking the air for the scent of dead meat.

Real trees. There must *be water down here.* I get so absorbed in looking for a creek, a puddle, anything wet, I forget to watch for stuff Gonzo might crash into—like the cluster of skinny rock towers straight ahead.

I look up at the last second. "Gonzo! Look out! Just ... STOP!"

Gonzo flares his wings and slams on the air brakes. The force rolls him backward into a stall. Before Gonzo can recover, he tumbles out of control and drops sideways into a cottonwood tree.

I'm surprised how it pains me to see this master flier bumble out of the sky.

Gonzo thumps from branch to branch, spills out of the leaves, and face-plants on top of a dead donkey.

"*Ay, caramba!* Are you tryeeng to keel me, Weemp?"

I glance up at the jagged rock towers, then back to Gonzo, just a few wingbeats away. A thought hits me so hard, I have to land.

I just saved Gonzo's life.

"You're amazing, Gonzo," I say, afraid he might not see things my way. Afraid he might throw one of his mega-tantrums and finish me off.

Luckily, Gonzo's ego is bigger than his temper.

"What? You theenk so?"

"For sure! In this whole huge desert, you were able to zero in on one dead animal with just a few sniffs. That's incredible!"

Gonzo cocks his head at the tree above him, rhythmically opening and closing his beak. That's how he reads the glow in things. "I meant to do that."

Willo alights beside me. "You did?"

I bat her across the chest with one wing. "Of course he did."

"I call eet ... the Tree Tango," Gonzo says, taking a bow while flaring his tail and wings.

I gulp down a laugh as Gonzo sets upon the stinking corpse.

The two of us watch him eat for a while, getting more bored, hungry, and thirsty.

"I guess we'll go look for some water," I say.

Gonzo grunts, his head buried inside the donkey's rotting rib cage.

"*Buen provecho*," Willo says.

Another grunt.

I stare at her.

"Enjoy your meal."

"How much time did you spend with Peevo, anyway? Learning Spanish, I mean."

"Tons. Helps kill time when trapped all winter in the Refugium."

"But she's a *Guardian*! Why would you hang out with her?"

"She's different. Just 'cause you're born with gilded wingbars and funny feet doesn't mean you're a monster, does it?"

"Yeah, but what about—"

"You'd like her, Wisp. Actually, she reminds me a bit of you."

Something stirs in me, something deeper than that burning itch to hurry north.

I ignore it.

By the time Willo and I return to Gonzo, the sun is nearing the lip of the canyon. We've scoured the canyon floor and found nothing a nighthawk could eat or drink. The closest we got? A tiny patch of wet, smelly mud, which I'm sure was some kind of pee, and a couple of scorpions that were in no mood to be eaten.

Gonzo still has his head buried in the dead donkey, this time up its nose.

"Uh ... Gonzo," I say. "You finished yet?"

Gonzo pulls his head out and wipes his dripping beak on the donkey's hide. "I saved thee best till last," he says, clicking his beak. "It ees hard work but thees ees thee only way to get at thee brains."

"Yum," Willo says.

"Somebody else, I don't know who, reeped open the donkey for me. I should thank heem."

"We might have to keep looking for something to eat," I say. "I mean, somewhere else. It'll be dark soon and—"

"Wait. You like bugs, right?"

"Sure do, when we can find them."

Gonzo points his beak at the gutted rib cage. "Well, there's lots een there."

I take a deep breath and stick my head inside. Sure enough, the place is crawling with wall-to-wall blowfly maggots. Though I'd much rather catch bugs on the wing, I'm way too hungry to get fussy. Now *this* I can smell. The rotten stink of death and decay—honey to Gonzo, torture to me. But he'll be picking my bones, too, if I don't eat something soon. So I dive right in.

"Room for one more," I call to Willo. "Come and get it!"

"You're sick!" Willo cries. "What do you think we are, ravens?"

"Hey, cheeken-girlie!" yells Gonzo, his head covered in donkey brains. "You theenk I am blind *and* deaf? You got a problem weeth ravens?"

"Uh ... not at all, Gonzo," Willo says.

"Would you watch your beak, Willo," I hiss. "Unless you eat sand, this is the best food you'll see today."

We crowd inside the dead donkey's chest cavity, choking

down maggot after squirming maggot.

A few moments later, I hear Gonzo's voice. *"¡Ah, gracias!"*

I look at Willo. "What the—"

I slowly turn around to see a mangy coyote padding toward us, head low, eyes locked on mine.

Trapped.

"Gracias, señor, for sharing your donkey weeth us."

The coyote is not impressed with Gonzo's fancy talk. He springs after him.

"Where'd he go?" Willo whispers.

"Shhh. Let's get out of here."

Whuhh-whuhh-whuhh-whuhh-whuhh.

Before we can scrabble our way out, the coyote leaps back into view, running in the opposite direction with his bushy tail tucked between his legs and a raven on his ass.

"You might theenk about getting out of there," Gonzo says when he returns, looking pretty proud of himself. "You must not trust a coyote."

"Like a raven, you mean?" Willo says as she climbs out and shakes blood and guts off her feathers.

"Of course," Gonzo says slyly.

"There's still the problem of water," I say, trying to keep the team spirit alive. After all, Gonzo just saved our lives.

So far today, it's one for one.

"Deed you check up there?" asks Gonzo, tilting his head toward a long, narrow cave. He's doing that beak thing again.

I hadn't thought of checking the canyon walls for water. "Are you, like, getting some water vibes from up there?"

Gonzo takes off without answering and makes a perfect beeline for the cave mouth.

"Do you think he's faking this blind act?" Willo asks. "I mean, look at him go!"

I shrug my wings. "Maybe he hears water fairies singing his name. Whatever works. I'm dying of thirst."

We launch after Gonzo and land at the cave mouth. I almost take off again when I see a cluster of mud huts perched on the cave floor. After that rock-happy kid in Puebla, I'm in no mood to mess with humans.

But the huts are empty. Some of their walls have collapsed and the ones still standing are cracked and crumbling. All abandoned, except ...

"Look!" I whisper to Willo. "A human in the window."

"You're hallucinating."

"No, really. An old man. Wrapped in a blanket. Long gray hair."

"You're just dehydrated."

"Maybe," I say. "But this is one spooky place."

"Where's Gonzo?"

"Good question. Gonzo! GON-ZO!"

21

CORNERED

Canyon de Chelly, Sonoran desert, Arizona

M y calls for Gonzo are met with a *koo-koo, koo-koo* from the back of the cave. "¡*Aquí!* Over here."

I draw on my night vision to fly deeper into the cave. I can just make out a familiar dark shape perched beside a still pool.

"*Gracias,* Gonzo," I say, slurping down beakfuls of sweet, cool water. "We never would have found this."

"Sure, we would've," Willo says.

I pause between slurps. *No way,* I think. *That's twice today Gonzo's saved us.*

"Bump into any ghosts up here?" I ask him.

"Not exactly, but I can tell you, we are not alone."

"Huh?"

"Leesen."

I catch the distant yapping of a coyote.

"Him again?"

"No. He ees just happy to get his dead donkey back. *Leesen.*"

Below the yapping, I detect the thumping of my heart. Then, drifting down from the cave's ceiling, a soft rattling sound, like bones rubbing together.

"What is it?"

Before Gonzo can answer, I hear another sound that makes me wince. The staccato flaps of approaching nighthawks.

The sound of rushing wings fills the air. All but one of the birds stay aloft, forming an aerial shield over the mouth of the cave. A lone nighthawk, biggest of them all, flutters casually to the top of the tallest hut.

Flare.

The squadron commander shouts into the darkness. "Wisp! By Royal decree, we have come to escort you home!"

I stop breathing.

Willo shakes beside me.

The rattling sound above us builds.

"Gonzo! I bring greetings from Plumablanca."

Gonzo pulls his head tight into his shoulders.

"Your leader says you are forgiven. He says, they miss you. Please come home soon."

"*Ay caramba,*" Gonzo grunts.

"How did he find us?" Willo squeaks. "What can we do?"

I flip a wing over her beak. "You, for one, can shut up."

Gonzo does anything but. Piercing whistles and whines escape from his magic throat. The sounds seem to spring from the other side of the cave.

Gonzo the ventriloquist. Freaky.

Flare turns his head in that direction.

I can't believe my ears. "How'd you *do* that?" I whisper.

Gonzo shrugs and throws another sound across the cave. *"Queek-queek! Queek-queek!"* The alarm call of a nighthawk in distress.

Where in the world did he learn that?

Flare points a wing at a crumbling hut where the sound seems to come from. "Guardians! Surround them! Flush them out!"

The aerial shield around the cave mouth collapses and a net of nighthawks is thrown over the hut.

Gonzo to the rescue—again! This makes no sense but I'll take it.

"Now!" he whispers. "Thees way!" And he bolts for the opposite end of the cave mouth. He narrowly misses crashing into several huts on the way out.

I enjoy a few wingbeats of sweet freedom until I hear the dreaded war cry of Flare's squadron.

"Kill-ree! Kill-ree!"

I look back and my stomach curdles. The whole pack of them is pouring out of the cave, straight for us, like a swarm of angry wasps.

Maybe we can ditch them in the dark, I think. That's another way Plebes have it over Guardians, who have lousy night vision even for nighthawks. Then I remember last night's full moon. Almost blinding. Tonight's moon is already rising, blood-red.

I figure our odds of escape are about zero, maybe less.

Flare's squadron gains fast.

I turn to Gonzo, panting beside me. "What are *you* worried about?"

"I am not afraid of a few measly cheeken-hawks. But eef those guys peck your eyes out, how can I find thee careeboo place?"

I have to laugh in spite of the ice in my blood. Just as I start wondering what Gonzo will do when Flare catches Willo and me, I hear shrieks of terror from the big, scary Guardians.

I look around to see another much larger swarm swooping down on the squadron. "Who the heck are they?"

"*Who-hah-hah.* The only ghosts I saw in that cave were bats. Ghost-faced bats. I've seen them in the cleefs above my beach."

The Guardians scatter in all directions, clumps of bats tailing each bird.

"You know, those bats, they like to follow *chotocabras.*"

"Why?" Willo asks.

"Because they theenk bug-eaters like you will lead them to good bug peekneek."

"Guardians hate bats," I say, laughing.

"Oh, that ees too bad. They weel be on their butts all night."

"Too bad for them," I say, feeling my whole body unwind. "Good for us."

I steer us along the lip of the canyon. I have this hazy feeling it runs due north. Instead of looking to the stars to confirm this—what a joke that would be—I close my eyes for a few wingbeats. At first, nothing. I scrunch my eyes tighter and really concentrate. There it is again, what I felt back in Mexico, that faint tug on my brain. It's like there's a little hole in the front of my skull with a thin jet of cool wind blowing through it. Arctic wind. It draws me forward, pointing me due north.

A happy glow floods my body. I realize this must be what Dad called an "inner navigator." How did he put it? *More reliable than even the stars.* It's like my inner navigator is just beginning to hatch, trying to peck through a thick shell of worries, doubt, and dread.

"Wisp!" Willo cries. "What are you doing?"

I open my eyes just in time to dodge a huge slab of rock sticking out from the top of the canyon.

"Uh ... just checking directions."

"Have you gone blind again? The Boreal star's dead ahead."

Yes! I think, though I don't bother looking for it. What's the point? I've found something else to steer by.

Besides, stars scare me. I think they remind me too much of my dead father.

We fly on in silence until one question starts tapping away at my brain like a woodpecker's beak. "How did Flare find us way out here?"

"That coyote must have ... how you say ... ratted on us," Gonzo says.

"Who's this Pocahontas character that Flare mentioned?" I ask.

"You mean, Plumablanca. Beeg macho boss of my beach. Your fat friend must have talked to heem, too. I tell you, that cheeken-hawk ees lucky to be alive."

The tapping in my head stops. "I bet Flare asks everybody along the way, 'Seen any nighthawks?' He knows it's still early for nighthawks to migrate, so—"

"You mean, like, for *normal* nighthawks," Willo says.

"Okay, *sheep* nighthawks. Anyway, if somebody says, 'Yep, they went that-away,' then Flare knows he's on our tail. Even with all his fancy training, I'm thinking that's his real secret weapon."

"What?"

"Interrogation."

"So?"

"So ..." A plan leaps out of my brain fog. "So, we talk to nobody. We fly only at night. Stay low. Avoid all major landmarks."

"Like, this canyon maybe?" Willo says.

"Uh ... right." I pull up and over the edge.

"But I'm tired," Willo says. "Can't we just—"

"We have to keep going, make some distance between us and Flare. We won't be safe till we get to the Tundra."

Gonzo slips into a relaxed barrel-roll. *"Lo qué sea."*

I look at Willo. "Huh?"

"Whatever."

We fly fast and low over the moonlit desert. As serene as it is, I'm praying for clouds. Thick, dark clouds to swallow the moon. Out here in this brightness, my keener night vision gives us no advantage over Guardian goons. With no place to hide, I feel like we're sitting ducks, just begging Flare to pick us off.

22

PEEVO
Panama beach

The crippled mallard doesn't have a chance. Peevo's raven guard grunts hungrily beside her as the duck flies low over the beach, her injured left wing carving random pockmarks in the sand. It makes a wobbly landing and tumbles into the surf. Plumablanca explodes after it with the rest of the mob on his tail.

A cloud of ravens descends on the duck. They form a tight circle just out of range of its stabbing bill. They croak and screech and snap their bills while Plumablanca spirals above them. The duck tries to flap away but, the instant its webbed feet leave the sand, Plumablanca knocks it flat. With one swift peck, he drives his bill into the duck's eye. The other ravens hop forward and take turns impaling the duck's head and neck until its body stops thrashing and blood spatters the beach.

Peevo's guard can't contain himself and takes a few tentative hops toward the duck party.

Now or never, Peevo thinks. She lunges toward the cliff, hoping for a camouflage advantage against the gray-brown rock. She trims her wings for a silent sprint.

But she has underestimated her captors.

With the same speed that Plumablanca pounced on the duck, he throws his full weight on top of Peevo, almost breaking her back. "You're next, goofy-hawk. Where do you theenk you are going?"

"Just stretching my wings," Peevo says, looking up into Plumablanca's eyes that flash white with every blink.

"Not funny."

"You know, sir, I was thinking," Peevo says, struggling to regain her diplomatic voice.

"You should be *praying* eenstead," he says, spilling drops of duck blood in her eyes.

"Not to seem discourteous or anything, sir, but I believe your plan to wait for my squadron to return with your runaway raven and our two rebels may be flawed."

Plumablanca puffs up his head and neck feathers until his body appears double in size. "All the more reason to eat you."

"Sir, I can offer you something much better."

The big raven cocks his head. "I don't care what my great-grandmother ate. Birds I can catch. Not feesh."

"No, sir. I am talking about more birds to eat. *Many* more. Specifically, ducks."

Plumablanca slowly backs off. "What do you chirp about, big-talker goofy-hawk?"

Peevo stands up and shakes the sand from her feathers. "I have heard that when your fish-eating ancestors ruled this beach, flocks of ducks would darken the sky every migration. They felt safe migrating through here, protected by the white-feathered ravens."

"But we steel get a few birds."

"Not like the old days."

"What happened?"

"For some reason, your ancestors lost the knowledge of how to fish. They had to switch to some other food."

"Birds."

"Exactly. Naturally, they struck hardest on the biggest and meatiest of them all."

"Ducks."

"Yes, sir."

Plumablanca's eyes turn to slits. He snaps his bill. "And the *juui-ciest*!"

"Yes, their meat is loaded with fat. But tell me, sir, do you see many ducks on your beach these days?"

Plumablanca looks back at the mallard, now just a smear of blood, bones, and feathers. "*No mucho*. Just eenjured or seeck ones like that." He tips his massive beak to the sky as streams of hungry, white-flecked ravens descend on the dead duck from all directions. "It ees not much to feed so many."

"When your ancestors turned from allies to enemies, ducks detoured around the mountains and flew over Venezuela instead. They've been migrating that way ever since."

"So now we get only leetle birds. Why ees that?"

"They don't have the muscle power to fly the long way around. They have to go over the mountains. But, sir, why chase little warblers and sparrows up and down the beach, not to mention nighthawks, when you could be feasting on hundreds of fat ducks?"

Plumablanca sizes up Peevo and shakes his head. "True, it ees a lot of work for not much food."

"And why risk getting squashed by a car while picking at road-killed lizards or getting shot while raiding dumpsters?"

The raven shrugs. "That ees how we must survive. There ees no other way."

"Ah, but there is, sir."

Plumablanca looks pointedly at Peevo, eyes wide. "So, how can leetle you help us?"

"I have connections in many bird cultures. I know how they work, how they think, how to spark stories that spread like wildfire. Release me and I promise to return to the Amazon and spread a *new* story about you far and wide."

"And that ees?"

"That the white-feathered ravens at the end of the mountains have returned to their fishing ways. That the faster flyway leading to this beach is safe for ducks once more. If you let me free, I will be living proof that they need not fear your clan ever again." Peevo lowers her head. "Of course, what you do with the ducks when they arrive is your business."

"Why should I believe that you weel do this theeng for us?"

"If I spread this good news and get ducks flowing your

way again, all I ask in return is that you make peace with us nighthawks."

Plumablanca spreads his shoulders, flashes his eyes. "And eef you don't?"

"Then we will just have to take our chances flying through here, won't we?"

"You will send me the juicy ducks?"

"You have my word," Peevo says, with her tail feathers crossed behind her back. "Their full-on migration will not begin for a couple of weeks. I can light a lot of fires in that time."

"What about your *Capitan*?"

"He will thank me for making peace with you."

"That ees, if you send me the ducks."

"I have promised."

"And the crazy vagrant you chase?"

"Wisp? Why eat him when you can feast on ducks? He is our business. We have many ways to punish him."

Plumablanca steps away from Peevo and idly taps the sand with both wingtips. "Maybe I weel take up feeshing in the meantime."

"You won't regret this, sir," says Peevo, fighting back an inner gush of triumph. "*¡Adios!*" She flutters upward until level with the cliff top. She tips her wings to the swelling mob of ravens on the beach, then cuts a clear path south, back toward the mountains and beyond, to her Colony still wintering in the Amazon.

Once Peevo is over the cliff and safely out of sight of the ravens, she does a swift one-eighty turn and bears due north, following in the wingbeats of Flare's squadron.

23

MUDPOT

Yellowstone National Park, Wyoming

"**Finally,** careeboo!"

I have to chuckle. "Uh ... not quite, Gonzo. A little big for caribou." *Like, five times too big.* Tall grasses tickle my belly as we weave through a herd of grazing bison.

I had expected Gonzo to crash into a lot more stuff after I insisted we fly so low. He flies now with his beak open most of the time. Says it helps him focus on the glowy stuff given off by living things. Since leaving the desert, he's had a few near-death crashes with things that don't glow, like a wind generator, a huge chicken statue beside a restaurant, and a highway billboard advertising Disneyland—the castle towers sticking above it almost killed him.

Gonzo might have splatted against any of this stuff if I wasn't always looking out for him, shouting warnings, telling him which way to turn. Willo accuses me of getting too buddy-buddy with him, wondering why I don't just let Gonzo kill himself. She says that once we guide him to the Tundra, he'll have no more need for me and will turn around and eat us. Then I remind her how he's saved us from more than one predator, including a hungry coyote and a mad Guardian named Flare. Besides, I'm still learning aerobatic tricks from him. The other day it was a hammer-head stall. Never even saw Dad do one of those. If Willo would only try stuff like this she might get on better with Gonzo.

I have to pull up fast to avoid hitting a big white bus. Fortunately Gonzo is right on my tail or he would have splatted into it. Willo flutters above a huge bison about to step in front of the bus. "Hey, look out, you big goof!"

I hear the threatening clack of Gonzo's beak. "Who are you calling a goof?" he snaps.

"Not you, Gonzo. The bison. Look out!"

The bull ignores her and moseys onto the road like he owns it. The bus blasts its horn and screeches to a stop within a feather's width of the bull's bum. Without looking back, he raises his tail and sprays the front of the bus with poop. A group of female bison and their calves join him, blocking the whole road. A long line of honking cars forms behind the bus.

I ignore the craziness and fly on, due north. At least I've got *that* direction down. Like listening for a faint sound or peering at a dim light, I've learned how to focus on that subtle wind in my skull that draws me north. Nobody taught me this. Like Dad said, it's my inner navigator. *It's in your blood, Wisp. Only you can free it.* It's like I have a new secret. I even let myself think it will wipe out my other secret—that

I can't read stars. I have to test this growing power, refine it, play with it like I do with my flying tricks.

Then my inner doubter kicks in. How far can I trust my newfound sense of direction? Could it lead me to a fatal wrong turn? Will it work for me when we get beyond the Boreal and I have to pick a safe route to the Tundra? To stay clear of the giant raven, I mean—if it even exists.

The giant raven. That will be my real test.

These thoughts carry me far from the road until I hear Gonzo shouting for me. "Hey, not so fast, Weemp!"

I look back and see him circling over the road-hog bison.

"Somebody, I hope, ees going to get run over!" he says.

I reluctantly wheel around. "I thought you were sick of eating roadkill."

"Seek of *stale* roadkeel, yes. Fresh roadkeel, no!"

A mob of humans pours out of the bus, holding up little square boxes and pointing them at the bison.

Gonzo squawks at the humans. They all point their boxes at him. He swoops down on a little boy and nimbly plucks away his red cap.

The boy screams.

Something spooks the bison. They leap off the road and stampede across the meadow.

A big grizzly bear blasts out of the grass and charges across the road.

Now *all* the humans scream and scramble back inside the bus.

The grizzly gallops after the bison.

Gonzo flaps after the grizzly.

I tag along after Gonzo, hoping he'll get a good feed so we can keep pushing north.

The bison herd runs headlong for a creek halfway across the meadow. Steam curls above the rushing water. Here and there, powerful jets shoot high into the air with a great whoosh. Beside the creek are pools of flying mud that bubble and belch as if the Earth were suffering from serious indigestion.

"So, like, what *planet* is this?" Willo asks.

It dawns on me that by fixing on a single bearing since leaving the desert—due north—we're now way off the main flyway. Good for ditching Flare. Bad for knowing where the heck we are. Willo never went through here on her way south. Me, neither. Only the winds know where I went. Since we left the Coco River back in Columbia, I've had to lean on Willo for almost every direction and landmark. Looks like those days are over.

We could get seriously lost.

"Beats me," I say, trying to hide this new fear. That's when I realize I better get my navigational act together real quick.

"Strange place," is all Willo says.

The grizzly zeros in on a calf desperately trying to keep up with the other bison. The herd storms across the creek, kicking up a huge spray of water and steam. The calf leaps out of the creek, then stumbles headfirst into a churning mudpot. After a few pathetic bleats, he sinks out of sight except for one tiny hoof that thrashes once, twice, then goes still. The bear charges after the retreating herd.

Gonzo swoops down and lands on the dead calf's hoof. *"¡Ow-chihuahua!"* He launches instantly, his wingtips flicking hot mud. He chases after the closest living thing around.

Willo.

"Why deedn't you tell me thees mud ees on fire?" he roars. "I could have been boiled alive!"

I watch in horror as Gonzo snaps viciously at Willo's rump. "Hey, cut that out!" I yell.

"*Ouch!*" Willo yells.

Gonzo swoops in front of her and spits a beakful of tail feathers in her face. "Next time, I go for your cheeken meat!"

I dive-bomb Gonzo's head. "Stop picking on her! It's not her fault you boiled your feet." I circle back and line up for another dive.

Gonzo flips on his back and thrusts his talons at my face. "Okay then, so I blame you! *Krrr-ok, krrr-ok!*"

A deep rumble from the mudpot breaks up the fight. The three of us hover side by side, staring down at it. Another rumble then, with one ginormous belch, out pops the half-poached calf. It lands with a *thunk* on a bed of orange poppies.

Gonzo plunks down beside the steaming carcass.

I perch on a nearby hump of wet rock. Like most everything else along this creek, the rock is making funny gurgling noises. "So ... uh ... how long will it take you to eat that thing?"

"Let eet cool down first," Gonzo says, lightly touching the calf with his wingtip. "Then I theenk the eyes and brains should do me."

I've seen this act many times on our long journey from Panama. Perfectly camouflaged against the gray-brown rock, I place my body so I can keep an eye on Willo, who has taken cover in a pine tree across the creek, and on what I now know to be the southern sky, watching for a squadron of hunting Guardians. Gonzo is hard at work, ripping out eyeballs and brains, looking blacker than black in a shroud of sunlit steam.

The hot, moist air, the long day's flight, and the excitement of chasing Gonzo off Willo's tail, all weigh heavily on my eyes and I fall into a daytime trance.

Amidst all the whooshing and bubbling noises, I fail to hear the staccato flaps of an approaching nighthawk until it's right over me. I don't see it until the moment it sets down on Gonzo's side of the creek. As it folds its wings, I catch the unmistakable glint of gilded wingbars.

My wings stiffen. *He's found us at last!* I fight the impulse to flee. I press tight against the rock knowing that staying invisible could save my life.

What about Willo? I squint through the steam at the branch where she landed. It's shaking.

The lone nighthawk bows to Gonzo. "Greetings from the Amazon, good sir."

That voice. I know that voice. I risk lifting my head. *Way too small for Flare.* A chunk of meat drops from Gonzo's beak as he cocks his head at the nighthawk.

"What is weeth you crazy cheeken-hawks? Aren't you supposed to be afraid of us?"

"I come in peace, sir. Only to ask you one question."

"Hmm. Let me guess. Have I seen any other *chotocabras* like you? Right?"

The nighthawk stands up to its full height.

Pretty dinky for a Guardian, I think. *Who is that?*

"Quite right, sir. Precisely the reason for my journey."

Gonzo opens his beak and looks directly at the rock where I'm hiding, then up at Willo's tree. My insides turn to bubbling mud. I will my legs to stop trembling. They don't.

How far can I really trust that raven? I guess I'm about to find out. I'm wishing now I hadn't yelled at him earlier.

"And what eef I have?" Gonzo says slowly.

"Well, sir, it is still too early for our kind to start the North Crossing. But two young vagrants escaped from our colony and are suspected of migrating to forbidden territory beyond our normal breeding range."

"And what ees so horreeble about that?"

"Our authorities believe they will set a bad example for others, especially our youth. They may pose a serious threat to the unity of our Colony."

"Do you believe thees?"

"I have my orders, sir."

Gonzo starts hopping from one foot to the other.

He does this when he gets impatient. Or hungry. Or both.

"What business ees all thees to me?" he asks, leaning over the mysterious nighthawk.

"The two vagrants are believed to be migrating in the company of a raven."

"I theenk you are being rideeculous. Ravens don't migrate."

The nighthawk swivels its head and glances in my direction.

It's only a glance but I feel sure I've been spotted. Like we locked eyes. In the same terrible moment, a light goes on in my brain. I totally know who this is.

Peevo.

Peevo looks back at Gonzo. "Then I suppose, sir, that would make three vagrants."

Gonzo hops on top of the dead, eyeless calf. He spreads his wings and throws the nighthawk into shadow. "What!

You say I am a vagrant? Now I *know* you are rideeculous! I say you *vamos* out of here fast before I pluck your eyes out!"

Peevo zips into the air. "Thank you, sir. You have been *most* helpful."

Gonzo clacks his beak and hops back and forth until his feet blur. His throat hackles swell, revealing a ring of white feathers.

Peevo abruptly breaks her spiral climb and circles overhead. She studies Gonzo. "I neglected to tell you, sir. The raven I mentioned comes from a certain white-feathered clan that is descended from bald eagles."

"Bah!" Gonzo says, scrunching his neck into his shoulders, as if to hide it.

"It is said they once ate only fish and became protectors of smaller birds that passed through their territory."

Gonzo hurls a volley of rasping *caw-caw-caws* at Peevo.

"Perhaps you will have news of such a raven if our paths cross again. *Muchas gracias, Señor.*"

"*Krrr-ok, krrr-ok.* Get out of my life, cheeken hunter!"

I close my eyes as if to be less visible. I'm sickened by the memory of Peevo giving Willo secret Spanish lessons last winter. *You want to talk about buddy-buddy, Willo? That was just plain weird.*

Or was it?

It dawns on me why Peevo might have spent so much time with her. The smartest, fastest, trickiest Guardian in the Colony befriended my little sister only to pick her brains and find out everything she could about *me*.

And here's Peevo now, a few wingbeats away, peering down at me before flying back to her squadron to report the good news.

Their hunt is finally over.
She's found the gang of vagrants.

24

CAPTURED
Calgary, Alberta

It's tearing me apart—all this zigging and zagging, up to the mountains, down to the prairies, back and forth for thousands of wingbeats. That burning itch is hotter than ever, scorching my heart. *Get to the Tundra as fast as you can!*

But no. We can't risk it. It's too dangerous.

Everything changed when Peevo popped out of the blue and landed right beside us. Even though we'd flown low to the ground, talked to no one, traveled mostly at night, I now understood a key flaw in our escape plan.

Flying due north was too predictable.

I figured that Peevo, fastest of the Guardians, had been sent to scout ahead. Her special buddy-buddy knowledge of Willo and indirectly, me, probably helped Flare figure out our route. Willo was as stunned as me to see Peevo. But she can't get her head around the fact that Peevo is part of a goon squad after our blood.

So we have to keep Flare guessing. We have to fly this wonky route that no bird in its right mind would follow.

None of us likes the idea, least of all Gonzo. "Weemp!" He yells as, for the tenth time today, I steer us on a ricochet course away from the mountains down to the prairies. "You are begeening to really peess me off. You drag me on thees wild goose chase so you can peek maggots off my body when I starve to death?"

"Or smash into another giant chicken statue?" I yell, dashing from side to side to confuse Gonzo even more. "Or telephone pole or mountain? How'd you like it if I stop warning you about stuff like that? See how long *you'd* last. Yum! Fresh maggots, here we come!"

Hollow popping noises shoot from Gonzo's beak. "Oh, yeah, cheeken-fart? Now I know that only loco birds migrate!"

Willo squeezes between us. "Would you guys stop your beak-flapping? We're going to need all our breath to fly around that city up ahead."

I open my beak to snap at my sister but clamp it shut when I spot a bright orange halo on the horizon. "What city?"

"Calgary. Biggest city on the Canadian prairies."

Since nightfall, we've been flying much higher than normal to avoid the crazy wind screaming out of the mountains. I straighten our course and take us up another thousand wingbeats to get a better view.

What I see takes my breath away.

"It's ... it's like an ocean," Willo gasps. "A huge twinkly ocean."

We're soon flying over wave after wave of orange lights. "Wow," I say. "That's a lot of humans."

"A lot of dumpsters!" Gonzo exclaims. "Let's dive een!"

"I have to agree with Willo on this," I say to Gonzo. "We'd be nuts to go right through town."

"Ah, but theenk of all the nice teedbeets down there. Doughnuts and cookies, French fries and cheezies—"

"And dogs and cats and raccoons to rip your beak off," I say.

"Yeah, but—"

"And humans with rocks and sticks and guns," Willo says.

"But I really like cheezies and—"

"And zillions of buildings and towers and wires to crash into," I add.

Gonzo falls silent.

I feel a drop of water on my head. Then another. I pull my eyes from the city lights. A mean-looking cloud is snuffing out all stars. Usually I crave starless nights. Not tonight.

"This is not good," I say.

A few more wingbeats, and we're flying through stinging rain. "You may love junk food, but cities mean trouble. Especially at night in crappy weather."

Gonzo fades back, pretending not to hear.

I try different altitudes, different directions, but find only more rain, more wind. The city lights give the cloud a furry orange look as if some giant animal is trying to roll over and squash us. Hairy arms seem to sprout from the cloud. They wrap us in a tunnel of wind and shove us toward a blazing wall of skyscrapers.

"You change your mind so fast, Weemp?"

"Uh ... looks like we don't have much choice. The trick will be to blast through these buildings without getting scrambled alive."

"I'm scared," says Willo. "I can't turn. I can't do anything."

"It's okay," I shout. "This tailwind wants to screw us around. Don't let it!"

"I can't fight it!"

"Don't even try. Just go with the flow. Keep the back of your wings down. Flap only when you have to. Just steer. Like we did in the Andes."

"Weemp!" Gonzo shouts.

I glance over both shoulders. I see a glint of reflected light from Willo's eyes, but no raven. "Where'd ya go?"

"I deed not tell you but eet is hard to see your alive-glow in thee rain."

"Then get closer, right on my ass! Both of you!"

We all tuck together in a ragged line. The rain bats us closer to the skyscrapers, the tops of which are now swallowed by the furry cloud.

The lower we go, the more we get sucked into the insane brightness of the city. The rain bends and bounces the light all around us.

My head feels like it could fly off. My newfound sense of direction is blown to bits by the wind. It's all I can do to stay aloft.

In the thick of skyscrapers, I spot a circular tower with a round red cap. I'm close enough to see humans moving around inside. A little girl, her hands cupped against the sloped window, peers into the stormy night.

I envy her safety and warmth.

"Weemp! What are you doing? Are you trying to keel us?"

That's when I realize I've been spinning around the tower. "Sorry!"

I straighten our course and shoot for a gap between two office towers.

Bad decision.

The gap leads to a canyon of mirror-glassed buildings. The light bounces around worse than ever. I can't tell the difference between thin air and plate glass.

The pelting rain forces us deeper into the canyon, until we are almost skimming the roofs of honking cars and buses.

That's when I see it.

Another nighthawk.

In the blur of mirrored glass and flashing lights, I glimpse the perfect silhouette of a nighthawk.

The stranger flashes in and out of view. It's on my tail one moment. Gone the next.

We streak past a blinking sign that, for a wingbeat, frames the bird in stark detail.

My heart jumps to my throat.

Gilded wingbars!

As if knowing it's been spotted, the phantom bird vanishes.

I dare to look over my shoulder.

Just Gonzo and Willo, flapping through the chaos.

Did they see it? Did I see it?

I peer at the glass whizzing by.

Nothing.

"Look out!" Willo yells as I fly straight for a streetlight swaying in the wind.

I pull up at the last second, brushing the streetlight with my tail-feathers.

Smarten up! That was just a freaky reflection.

Then I remember the wingbars.

Just a trick of light on Willo's wings.

I spot a gap in the buildings, like a cave, stuffed with brightly lit trees. Humans sitting around below them, looking warm, dry, safe. "Over there!" I shout. "Go for the trees!"

I'm too scared to look back to see if Willo and Gonzo are still on my tail. I take aim at the trees and tilt my wings for maximum thrust. I swoop so low I startle a group of young humans rolling down the sidewalk on little boards.

They throw their arms over their faces. "Bats!" one of them yells.

I line up to blast into the lit-up trees. I don't care what's in there. All I know is it'll be better than this howling storm.

The wind tries to push me past the trees. I fight it with all my might until my flight muscles burn.

Just two hundred wingbeats to the trees.

"Weemp!"

One hundred wingbeats.

"Just follow me!" I yell. "Stay close!"

Twenty.

Powerful talons clutch my chest, almost puncturing my lungs. I hang upside down, my head limp. I can't see my captor. The horrible rush of muscular wings, beating so close to my head, drowns out the wind, the traffic, even the frantic cries of my sister.

25

TAILED
Calgary, Alberta

I'm dimly aware of my captor twisting and turning around buildings, streetlights, power lines.

Then I hear shouting far behind me.

"Gonzo! GONZO!"

Why is Willo calling for Gonzo?

"You let him go!"

What? So that's who has me in a death grip!

"Gonzo," I mumble. "What are you—"

"Shut up your beak," he snaps.

Never trust a raven! So the blind thing was a hoax after all.

I let my head flop backward and see Willo pumping after us with all she's got.

Gonzo dekes around a corner.

"*Ack-ack-ack!*" she screams. "You come back here!"

"Who-hah! Who-hah!"

He wants her to follow? Or is he laughing at her? What's going on?

Willo wheels around, fights her way back upwind, and charges after us. We shoot out of the canyon of office towers toward a ribbon of darkness that snakes out of town.

Willo finally gains on us and starts dive-bombing Gonzo's head. "Let go of Wisp, you big bully!"

My gutsy sister.

"Hey, cheeken-brains, you are geeving me a headache!"

"Drop him!"

"Okay, eef you say so."

I feel his mighty talons release me and I drop like a rock into the black.

It takes a moment to find my lungs again, my brain, my wings. I take a few feeble flaps, then pull into a hover.

"What are you doing?" Gonzo yells. "Thees is maybe not a good time for a sweem."

As my eyes recover from the city's blinding glare, I make out the tree-lined banks of a river. A few wingbeats away, my awkwardly hovering sister.

"You better keep working on that hover of yours," I say.

Willo spins circles around me. "You're not dead!"

"Not that I know of. Just got a little winded when a certain deranged raven attacked me." I lunge at Gonzo who circles slowly above us. "What was that about, dumpster brains?"

"I theenk maybe you should learn to say *gracias*."

"For almost killing me?"

"Weemp, you almost keeled yourself."

"How, exactly?"

"Like scrambling your brains on the humans' glass nest."

"But ... I was going for that cave of trees. It seemed like a safe roost to wait out the—"

"There were no trees."

"What?"

"No cave, either."

"How would you know?"

Gonzo flaps over to a cottonwood tree beside the river and lands on the highest branch. Willo and I perch several wingspans away. The whole tree rocks in the wind.

"You kept yelling about trees," Gonzo continues, "but I deed not sense any inside."

"You mean, no, what-cha-call, loosey-goosey stuff?" I say.

"*Luz de vida?* The alive glow? *Nada.* Only humans inside. If you saw trees, they were *falso* ... how you say... fake."

"So what about the cave?"

"Use your brain, Weemp. Do you really theenk humans would poke big holes in their fancy nests?"

"Uh ... I guess not. But maybe next time you could, like, warn me instead of bashing into me and squeezing me to death!"

"I tried, but you are pretty stubborn cheeken-hawk. *Who-hah!* And fast. You would not leesen. I had to grab you before you crashed into thee glass."

"I think you're faking this blind act," Willo says.

We agree on this one, Willo.

Gonzo turns and looks squarely at her, his eyes ablaze with reflected streetlights.

Willo puffs up her breast feathers. "So, just how did you zip so fast around all those buildings?"

"That is seemple. These big human nests, they are buzzing."

"You mean, like a bug?" I ask.

"No, cheeken-brain. They glow."

"But I thought you only saw living stuff."

"So deed I. But I theenk I am getting better at this."

"So what do you see?"

Gonzo looks up through the rain at the glowing office towers. "It ees not like *luz de vida*, not swirly and pink like in birds and animals. Whatever buzzes through these nests ees fainter, mostly blue and green." Gonzo lifts a wing and moves it sideways then up and down. "It runs in straight lines through the walls, the floors, all over. Outside in the wires, too. Thees I can see even in the rain."

The anger in me shrivels. We sit silently on the swaying branch surrounded by roaring traffic and hissing rain.

Gonzo faces the towers.

I watch Willo, whose eyes are fixed on Gonzo. *She still doesn't trust him. I don't blame her.*

"I'm losing count," I say.

"Huh?" Gonzo grunts.

"Of how many times you've saved us."

Long pause.

Gonzo shrugs. *"Yo también."*

Another pause. "Well?" I say to Willo.

She keeps staring at Gonzo. Still really angry. "He said, 'Me too.'"

I decide not to mention the nighthawk I saw in the glass. It had to be Willo. *Why get her more upset about nothing?* "Let's get out of this loony bin," I say.

"Bueno," Gonzo says.

We launch, one-two-three, from the cottonwood and fly low over the river. This time, Willo sticks close to my tail. Gonzo brings up the rear, breathing down Willo's back.

We fly until the city is nothing but an orange smudge on the southern horizon. Until a crack of light to the east announces a new day. Until Willo and I are flying side by side, half asleep. I have no idea where Gonzo is and, in my pooped state, I don't care.

I first hear it high above the prairie farmland, as if in a dream.

The staccato flap of another nighthawk.

The sound folds itself into my drowsy brain. With half-closed eyes, I imagine flying high over the bald Tundra. Willo and Dad dip and dive around me. Our silent joy, our total freedom, lift me up, carry me higher and higher until I feel weightless and alive like never before.

The staccato flap gets louder, closer.

I open my eyes wide.

Not Tundra, but prairie.

Not Willo. Not Dad. I know their flaps like my own.

Who?

Before I can look over my shoulder, another nighthawk effortlessly sculls up beside me. There's just enough dawn light for me to make out the flash of gilded wingbars.

My lungs fill with ice.

"Mind if I join you for a bit?" the Guardian asks.

26

FLARE'S PLAN
Alberta prairie

Gusty winds hammer Flare's squadron. Any weaker birds might be knocked clear across the prairies. But his crack team of Guardians punches through the turbulence, driven on by a constant stream of threats and abuse from their commander.

"If I can go three days without sleep, so can you!" Flare shouts.

"Of course, sir," says Striker, who as usual flies precisely two-and-a-half wing-lengths behind and to the left of Flare. Like the rest of the panting squadron members, he struggles to hold on to his assigned flight position.

Flare's punishing pace pushes the Guardians to the limit. His notorious diamond-shaped flock is beginning to fray at the edges.

"I should inform you, however," says Striker hesitantly, "that in this wind we are burning up our energy reserves approximately three times faster than normal."

"So what?"

"Well, sir, I fear that if we continue at this pace without a hunting break, we may face an increased risk of attack by—"

"That's a lot of crap and you know it. Ever seen a predator this high?"

"Well, no sir, but—"

"Exactly!"

"With all respect, sir, the lack of oxygen at this altitude may in fact be contributing to the squadron's weakened condition."

"Don't give me your twaddle, Striker. There's approximately three times *less* air resistance up here. What's the problem?"

"Fine, sir. But it may be very difficult to spot the vagrant nighthawks at this height. I suggest that if we descend for a hunting break, we could get a better—"

"Striker, let me remind you that *I* make the suggestions for this flea-bitten flock."

"I'm sorry, sir."

"Why do I train geeks like you? Why do I brief you? Don't you get it, wingnuts? Since those idiot bats chased us off his trail, our best chance of finding that vagrant is to race ahead and ambush him."

"Where, sir?"

"You're supposed to be piloting this squadron, for dirt's sake! You haven't figured that out yet?"

"Well, sir, traveling this far without the aid of Plebeian navigators leaves us with only major landmarks and wind currents to guide us. Your directive was that I advise you on the fastest flyway to the Boreal Forest. That indeed is the course I have tried my best to set."

"Well then, try harder! Just get us to the damned Boreal and leave the rest to me. I'll take us to a place migrant suckers like Wisp can't possibly resist."

"And that would be?"

Flare sweeps his wings up in disgust, causing a near pile-up of Guardians behind him.

"His nest site, you idiot!"

"Of course, sir. Yellowknife's Moosehead School."

"Brilliant, Striker!"

"But, sir, I understood he was planning to overshoot the Boreal and escape to the—"

"Tundra? The treeless fairyland that exists only in his juvenile brain?"

"Yes, sir, but his father Damon is said to have returned from—"

"His father was equally batty! I tell you, Striker, wherever the hell Wisp *thinks* he's going, the closer he gets to that school, that roof, that particular patch of gravel where he was so unfortunately hatched, the stronger will be the pull. It'll rip his guts out to skip on by." Flare holds his wings still for a moment. "Hmm, not an unpleasant state, come to think of it."

"What will you do to him, sir?"

"I'm working on that." Flare rocks his wings playfully. "Still devising his most befitting end."

"And, sir, his sister?"

"Throw her to the ravens. It's Wisp I want. That Arwen wants. All we need is some *evidence* of our capture."

"Sir?"

"Perhaps a bloodied feather ..." Flare pauses, starts to hum a cheery tune. "No, I think a leg or beak would be more convincing. We hand our prize over to Arwen and, *Kill-ree!* I'm Principal Guardian! My first duty? Kick the old dame off her stump and end this messy business of migration."

"Uh ... I beg your pardon, sir?"

"Wouldn't you agree that our queen has worked hard for us all, Striker?"

"Undoubtedly, sir."

"And wouldn't you say she deserves a long vacation, maybe even early retirement?"

"I suppose so, sir."

"You could have my old job as squadron leader."

"Well ... er ... thank you, sir."

"Once that battle-axe is gone, we establish the Amazon's first year-round Colony of nighthawks."

"You mean, sir ... we would *not migrate*?"

"You're finally showing some promise, Striker."

"But, sir—"

"But what?"

"Well, sir, migration is basic to our survival. It's as much a part of us as ... as our *feathers*!"

"Cute, Striker, but not true. Migration means death. Death by starvation, predation, storms, poisoning, crashing into towers and buildings. We lost almost half the Colony during last fall's South Crossing, Striker. Keep that up and in a few years ... well, you can do the math. You call *that* survival?"

"I don't know, sir, I—"

"It'll be good for the Colony, Striker. You'll see."

"But what about food, sir, all the insects we'll need?"

"When the supply of fire ants gets low inside, we allow closely supervised bug hunts beyond the Refugium."

"And, sir, all the space we'll need to nest?"

"We learn to nest side by side, bill to bill, in true community spirit. I've thought all this through, Striker. It's quite do-able, with the right birds in charge."

"And that would be?"

"Guardians, of course. Only we have the strength and discipline to usher in this new era of safety and abundance. After a few no-fly seasons, the idea of migrating every spring and fall, back and forth, suffering and dying, all that will become nothing more than a bad dream. Those who don't see the benefits for the Colony—"

"You mean, sir, those who don't obey?"

"That's right. We can expect some resistance from the Plebes."

"And the Royals, sir?"

"No doubt. The blind who can't see the benefits of a year-round Colony, who scoff at the idea, will be fed to maggots."

"Maggots, sir?"

"Yes, another secure source of food for all."

"Maggots."

"Yes, of course. They're quite delicious if you haven't tried them. I plan to establish maggot farms in and around the Refugium."

"Maggot farms."

"Yes, Striker. Maggot farms. They are the key to our colony's future. A safe and happy future rooted forever in the Amazon. Striker, I'm talking about the end of hunger. The end of migration. The end of suffering. The birth of true freedom for nighthawks. Guardian nighthawks, that is.

Besides maggot fodder, we'll have no use for Plebes."

"As navigators, you mean?"

"Correct, Striker. Who needs navigators when you don't need to go anywhere? Gradual Plebeicide may be the best way to serve the Colony's long-term interests."

"Plebeicide."

"Has a nice ring to it, don't you think?"

Striker slips several wing-lengths behind his commander. He drifts in stunned silence, wrapped in an airstream tainted by Flare's skunky breath. At the sound of Flare's voice, he shoots back into position.

"So you see, Striker, it's very, very important that we capture this vagrant."

"Understood, sir."

Flare clenches his beak. "Only then will I be made Principal Guardian. Only then will all Guardians be united under me. Only then will we rise up and gain the power to offer this great gift to the Colony. The gift of freedom!"

"Uh ... if you say so, sir."

"I know so, Striker. Trust me."

Flare's plan for a Guardian revolt leaves Striker gasping for air.

Not Flare.

The very thought of Wisp boosts his speed. He feeds off his hatred, gaining as much energy from it as a belly full of horseflies. He lifts his beak and leads the squadron higher yet, twenty, twenty-five, thirty thousand wingbeats above the prairie farmlands.

His eyes glaze over as he finally levels off. His oxygen-starved brain runs wild with visions of glory. Ambushing Wisp at Great Slave Lake. Clamping his big feet around his throat. Savoring Wisp's howls as he is forced to watch his sister's eyes plucked out by ravens. Feeding him to the maggots.

Flare's bright visions fade into black. His eyes shut completely. His heavy body tumbles out of control.

He is vaguely aware of strong wings braking his fall, ferrying him out of the sky, setting him down beside a prairie pond.

His head feels like it's been crushed by eagle claws. He winces to the grinding squeal of yellow-headed blackbirds. He opens his eyes to the whistling of duck wings.

A ring of stone-faced Guardians stares down at him.

"What are you gawking at?" he grunts. "Striker. Striker! Where are you?"

Striker flutters into view above the circle of gilded birds. "Right here, sir."

"What in dirt's name are we doing on the ground? You had strict orders to get us to the Boreal Forest as fast as goddamned possible!"

"Just checking for landmarks, sir. None in sight but I believe we're still on target."

"You *believe* we're on target?"

"Well, you know, sir, how difficult it is to navigate without Pleb—"

"Forget Plebes! They're steering for extinction. And it begins once we catch that Wisp. How long to Yellowknife?"

"At this rate, another couple of days, sir."

Flare flips his wings, tries to stand up, and teeters over.

Forty wings reach out to break his fall.

Flare pushes them away. "A couple of *days*? Striker, we have a very slippery vagrant to catch and no one's snoozing through the night. With a non-stop advance, we can cut our time in half. We're going to beat that loser at his own game. Are you getting the picture, Striker?"

"Understood, sir, but may I suggest we stop at this pond to feed. There's a fresh hatch of caddisflies and our progress can only improve if—"

"Suck it up, Striker. You can eat your fill when we have Wisp in our claws! Go grab me some of those caddisflies so I can fly us outta here."

"Right away, sir." Striker wheels shakily out of view.

Flare opens his beak to shout another order then clamps it shut when a dark form glides silently over the squadron straight for Striker. He hears a dull thud, an urgent rustling of dry cattails, then a nasty ripping sound.

The tearing of nighthawk flesh.

"Red-tailed hawk, sir," says Rearguard Lance who flutters just above the cattails. "Doesn't look good."

Flare manages to stand up. "Serves him right for defying orders," he grumbles. "Now, who'd like a promotion to Chief Investigator?"

27

SECRET PROJECT
Alberta prairie

It takes a few wingbeats for me to figure out who just caught up.

Peevo.

All I can say is, "You!"

Peevo looks past me with an odd grin. "Morning, Willo. *Que pasa?*"

"Like, scare me or *what*?" Willo says.

"I didn't mean to."

I look all around. Nothing but a big v of northbound snow geese and a mob of magpies picking at a dead dog. Bald prairie in all directions. No sign of Flare.

Or Gonzo.

"You alone?" I ask.

"Yep."

I squint hard at her.

Peevo shrugs her wings. "Be hard to hide a whole squadron of Guardians out here."

"That goon sent you?"

"Flare?" Peevo shakes her head. "Not really."

I lunge toward her, detecting the faint scent of sweetgrass. *Must be the prairie I smell.* "What do you mean?"

"Let's just call it … a secret project."

I can't tell who I'm talking to. Willo's buddy or Guardian spy? "Secret project. Like Willo's Spanish lessons?"

Peevo's grin widens.

I flare my wings and drop behind Peevo. "Was that *you* back there?"

Peevo does an easy circle around me. "Uh … where?"

"Calgary."

"You're a pretty hot flier. And that rain didn't help. I almost lost you in there."

"And back in that bison meadow, with all the steam. You spotted us?"

"In Yellowstone, you mean?"

So that's what it's called. "Uh … yeah."

"Did I spot Mr. Invisible? No. But Willo? How couldn't I? Her branch was shaking like a rattlesnake's tail."

Willo lets go a silly laugh.

This is insane, chit-chatting with a Guardian! "Just what is your game?"

"Got restless. Like you."

"Where's Flare?"

"Don't know."

"How do I know you don't know?"

Peevo laughs. "I know you know that I don't know."

"Cut it out. Where is he?"

"Where's Bonzo?"

"It's *Gonzo* and none of your business." *I wish I knew.*

"Hanging out with the dark side now, eh?" says Peevo.

"You Guardians *own* the dark side," I say.

"Tell that to Arwen."

"She treats you pretty good," Willo says, "sending you to Europe and all."

"Not bad, I guess."

"She must have big plans for you," Willo says.

"Yeah," Peevo says scarily. "Dark plans."

"What are you doing here?" I demand. "What do you want?"

"Company."

"Yeah, sure."

"That was a pretty bizarre route you guys took," Peevo says after a long pause. "I'm zig-zagged out."

"Didn't work," I say.

"Don't see Flare, do you?" Peevo says.

"*You* found us. One Guardian's as bad as twenty."

"You gave Flare's squadron the slip," Peevo says. "That's not easy."

"But you're *part* of his squadron."

"Was."

"You're lying!"

Peevo shrugs. "Okay. Don't believe me."

"Where is he?" I ask again.

"Haven't seen him since Panama."

Willo screws up her beak. "So, like, why didn't you catch up sooner if you wanted company so bad?"

"I wanted to be positive he wasn't on *my* tail."

"Which would ... lead him to us?" Willo says.

"You got it."

"Oh, thanks," I say sarcastically.

"You're welcome."

The three of us fly on in prickly silence.

I want to scream.

After another thousand wingbeats, I finally crack. "Would you just tell us what's going on?"

"I'm sorry if I scared you," Peevo says.

"You're sorry?" I say. "That's what Guardians *do*. Scare us Plebes so you can boss us around."

I grit my beak. My brain hurts. And not just because I haven't slept or eaten for two days. "So, like, you've been tailing us since Yellowstone, right?"

"Yep. Took me that long to find you. Flare was right about one thing. You are one slippery nighthawk."

"We escaped from your squadron *twice*," Willo says, "once over a volcano and again in a canyon."

Peevo shrugs her wings. "Looks like I got lucky. And it's Flare's squadron, not mine. I left it, remember?"

"Right," I say, increasingly suspicious. "Why did you dump them?"

"What does Flare need a translator for way up here?"

"Flare needs a translator to understand any word longer than three letters!" Willo says.

"That's not why you left," I say.

"Okay, so maybe I got sick of being razzed by other Guardians," Peevo says.

"You are kind of dinky for a Guardian," I say. I peek under Peevo's belly. That same sweetgrass scent. "Got the fat feet, though."

"They called me a Plebe-hugger," Peevo says. "A mutant."

I'm amazed at how Peevo sweeps through the air so effortlessly. "Could Flare even keep up with you?"

"Not a chance. Stuck me in the back of the squadron to pretend he was faster."

"I still think you're lying," I say. "Leaving a Guardian squadron makes you a—"

"Deserter, yep."

"Which is punishable by—"

"Death, uh-huh. But no worries. Flare figures I'm already dead."

"What?" Willo and I say together.

"I discovered an easy way out of the squadron. On a beach in Panama."

"Gonzo's beach?" I ask.

"Yep. We stopped there to ask a few questions and the ravens jumped all over us."

"Duh," I grunt.

"I offered myself as a hostage."

"A hostage," I say.

"Yeah. It was a perfect plan. The ravens keep me. They send the rest of the squadron to go find Gonzo."

"What for?"

"To deliver a message from the head raven."

"Which was?"

"Gonzo, come home!"

"Hah!" I say. "Fat chance Gonzo would ever go back to those toughs."

"Or that Flare would ever return for me," Peevo says.

"And *that* was your perfect plan?" Willo says.

"Sure. I make a clean break from the squadron. Flare

gives me up for dead. I weasel my way out of the ravens' talons. And *voilà*, I'm free to go look for you."

Willo frowns. "But once Flare was out of your face, why not just take off on your own?"

Peevo goes oddly silent for many wingbeats, then, "I told you already. I wanted company."

"The company of *Plebes*?" I ask.

"Not just any Plebes."

I look at Willo, bamboozled.

"Look," Peevo continues, "you might as well know. I want something you've got."

I flare my wings. "And that would be?"

"Freedom."

"Oh, that," I say, pulling away from her.

"The way you tell Arwen off," Peevo says. "The way you fly where you like, eat what you like, shape your own life. I want that."

I shake my beak like I'd swallowed something awful.

"Guardians may be bigger and stronger than you," Peevo says. "We may have the power to boss you around but—"

"Or try to," I say.

"Okay, *try* to. But we don't have any freedom. Not like you."

I moan. "Oh come on."

"I've watched you practicing your flight stunts."

"Until one of your fat cousins knocks me down."

"I've eavesdropped on your stories about your trip south, living as free as a—"

"*Bird*?" I say.

Peevo laughs. "Well, a *free* bird, anyway. I've heard that you talk to parrots, squirrel monkeys, even vampire bats."

"You talk to *vampire bats*?" Willo cries.

"Hey, they all taught me something," I say. "Matter of survival."

"You're everyone's friend, Wisp," Peevo says.

"Oh, spare me."

"Really. Guardians can't do that. We have strict orders to impose order. That's all we do. Impose order. How fun is that?"

I do a quick barrel-roll. *Where is that raven?* "Tons, I bet."

"Tons of *boredom*! Like you, I had to get out of there. I had to leave all that."

I'm struck dumb.

Then a little light goes on in my head. "So, like, I guess that makes us all vagrants?"

Peevo turns to me with a look that, for a flash, melts all my fears. "I prefer the term *vanguard*."

"What's that?"

Peevo raises her head. Her buffy breast feathers swell out and flutter in the wind. I catch that sweetgrass scent again. "Vagrants are accidents, flukes. Birds that get blown off course and end up in some random place. No plan. No freedom. Just playthings of the wind. But vanguards? They *choose* their own flyways. Explore amazing places. Show the way to new territories, to a better life. Vanguards are leaders, Wisp, like you."

I grunt. "That's a bunch of crap."

"I've heard the rumors, Wisp. I've heard you're flying to the Tundra."

"Alone ... *supposedly*."

"You believe in it?" Willo asks.

"I really do," Peevo says. "Midnight sun. Big sky. Zillions of bugs. The end of starvation. Sounds like a good destination."

I don't dare ask her about the giant raven.

"Uh ... did you happen to notice I'm not dragging the whole Colony along with me?" I say.

"There are other believers out there, Wisp. It won't happen all at once but they will follow you."

"What about the Third Oath?" Willo says. "You know ... *no life beyond the Boreal.*"

"Those Oaths are just Arwen bafflegab and everyone knows it. All that's crumbling. Your escape, your dream, your freedom give hope to others, Wisp. Who knows who's next? That's why you're so dangerous to Arwen."

It still rings in my ears. The grumble of Plebeian voices chanting the Three Noble Oaths.

"It might start with your family, a few others, then we're into a full-scale rebellion."

Sure, my family. You're probably looking at all that's left of it.

"Guardians, too?" asks Willo.

"If Guardians rebel first and Flare gets his way, migrating *anywhere* will be history. Plebeians, too, for that matter."

So old Tamas was right about Flare's plan. "You mean ... Plebeicide?"

Peevo looks far ahead, beyond the greening fields and endless fence lines. She nods imperceptibly. "Uh-huh. That's what he calls it. But you can stop him, Wisp."

"How, exactly?"

"For one thing, you can stay out of Flare's clutches. Next, you must prove that the Tundra is habitable for nighthawks."

And kill the giant raven while I'm at it. No problem.

"And last, you must get word to the rest of the Colony of your accomplishment. Someday, hundreds of nighthawks will be breeding on the Tundra, living in a new land of freedom and plenty, thanks to you."

"I'm going to puke," I say. "Is this your so-called secret project?"

"Not secret anymore," Peevo says.

I glare at Peevo, as afraid that she might be telling the truth as telling lies. A bomb goes off in my head. I realize that as a Guardian deserter, she can never return to the Refugium. She can never return to the Boreal. *She'll have to come with us to the Tundra. But is she a genuine deserter? What is she really up to?*

"What a pile," is all I can spit out.

"Whether you chose this role or not, Wisp, you're a leader."

I bolt ahead. "Come on, Willo."

Willo reluctantly falls in line behind me.

"You know I can track you," Peevo calls out to us. "I can find you."

"Get lost, Guardian freak!" I shout. "I lead nobody nowhere!"

"I see," Peevo shouts back. "So who's that following you?"

"She leeched on to me! Now I'm stuck with her." I don't mean to be that hard on Willo but I'm mad at the world right now.

I look up. *Where is he?* I do one barrel-roll then another.

From way above comes a high-pitched "*Squeerk! Squeerk!*"

A black speck streaks out of the clouds right for us. Gonzo, sliding bum-first out of the sky, like the first time I saw him.

He flips around, goes into a full tuck, and charges straight for Peevo.

I'm amazed how much I trust this raven. Right now, he's all we've got for protection.

Peevo doesn't flinch as Gonzo whizzes past, missing her by a feather.

"You signaled for me, *amigo*?" Gonzo says as he levels off beside me. "This cheeken-hunter trying to rough you up?"

"She's harmless," I say, so wishing that was true. "Got lost without a Plebe navigator."

"You want maybe that I peck her eyes out?" Gonzo says.

I tilt my wings for maximum thrust. "Forget her. No Guardian could possibly keep up with us."

But Peevo does keep up. She follows us like before, steadily, silently, almost out of view. For thousands of wingbeats. Flying high above the vast prairie, Peevo tails us like a phantom.

"*Perdóname*, Weemp, but thees ees just a leetle insane."

"Huh?"

"To keep flying and flying past breakfast!"

Willo huffs. "Like, *yesterday's* breakfast."

Gonzo swoops down on Willo and takes a big sniff.

"Hey!" Willo cries. "Bug off!"

"Just keeding, cheeken-face."

"You eat grass?" I ask.

"Very funny," Gonzo says. "I should have pecked that stranger's eyes out."

"You'd puke on Guardian meat."

"There better be *mucho* meat on the Tundra, Weemp, or you are een beeg trouble."

"Yeah, yeah, you'll see."

Clouds of mosquitoes and black flies swarm through my mind. My stomach goes wild. I've barely seen a bug since Calgary.

"I'm hungry, too, Wisp," Willo says.

"Keep flying."

My heart jumps to the sound of nighthawk wings racing up behind me.

"I know a place."

Guess who.

I drop into an inside loop and level off smack on Peevo's tail. "What are you talking about, Guardian freak?"

"A place where there's plenty of bugs and meat."

"We're not hungry," I say.

"Just pretending, were you?"

I had forgotten that little fact about Guardians. Lousy navigators. Amazing ears.

Gonzo wheels around and flips on his back right above Peevo's head. "What ees thees place, cheeken-hunter?"

"The Athabasca River. Squirming with bugs. Hopping with fish. If we veer northeast, we'll hit the river real soon, just as it enters the Boreal Forest."

"Why should we believe you?" I snap.

"I'm hungry, too. But humans have wiped out most of the bugs with some weird spray they dump on their crops."

No wonder so many nighthawks die out here.

"If we keep on your bearing, we'll starve."

"And can you even *guess* what bearing I'm on?" *Hey, it never hurts to ask directions, even from a Guardian.*

"Due north," Peevo says.

How about that. I must be getting better at this. No more zigzagging for me. "Who says we'll starve?"

"You've been here before?"

"Not exactly but—"

"Then let me show you around."

I pull ahead of Peevo, sticking to the same bearing, my beak clenched so tight it almost cracks.

"Your clan catches fish, right?" Peevo says.

What the—I turn around and see Gonzo still flying upside down above her. He flips right side up and thrusts his talons at her head. "Of course we do! Now take us to thees place before I make a feather sandweech out of you."

"Wait a minute, Gonzo," I cry, "Since when is *she* the leader around here?"

"You got better idea, Weemp?"

"Well, no, but she's a—"

"Then flap your weengs, not your beak!"

For the first time this trip, I take up position at the rear of our little flock. And what a strange flock it has become. A pint-sized, big-footed Guardian nighthawk with a blind raven breathing down her back. Trailing far behind, us two Plebes, totally running out of steam.

"Are you feeling it?" I ask Willo after flying in silence for a long time.

"Starved? Duh!"

"No, no."

"Half-dead?"

"No. I mean this ... this sick feeling. I can't shake it."

"What? What?"

I glide in close beside her, whispering, "That we're flying into a trap."

28

FISHING LESSONS
Athabasca River, Alberta

"You gotta love this place," Willo says.

I let go a big sigh. "Totally."

A thousand wingbeats below, the Athabasca River curls through a green mat of spruce and poplar trees. Gateway to the Boreal Forest. Like Peevo said. I still have no idea what her game is, but the place she's led us to looks pretty good to me now. Any lingering dread I had of flying into a trap is eclipsed by the promise of food.

"Supper!" I shout, feeling oddly lighter and happier than I have for days. I pull in my wings, go into a half-tuck. I shoot past Peevo, intent on ruffling her feathers, in a dead-drop plunge to the river.

On the way down, the wind screams through my tail

feathers and I hear a sound that blows open a flood of feelings for ... my father.

That sound of a male nighthawk defending his territory— or his mate.

"*V-R-R-R-O-O-O-O-M!*"

At the bottom of the dive, I give my head a quick shake. *Wait a sec. Was that me?*

My spine tingles.

My heart jumps.

It was me!

This is a thrilling first. Nobody taught me this trick. I don't even know how I made it. Was it the funny way I happened to spread my tail feathers? The angle of my dive? The speed of my descent?

Whatever.

"Hey!" Willo yells. "Wait up!"

This time I don't wait up. I don't look back. I'm on a roll.

I dip and dive over the river. I circle and swoop over the marshes. I gulp down hundreds of flying insects. The pickings are amazing. Crickets and caddisflies, black flies and beetles, moths and mosquitoes, and grasshoppers, too.

I see Willo and Peevo farther downstream, hunting together.

Meanwhile Gonzo's stomach is still grumbling. "Hey, you crazy *chotocabras*," he yells from the top of a giant spruce tree. "All those leetle bugs are fine for you. But I thought you promised lots of meaty theengs, too."

Peevo spirals up and boldly lands right beside him.

I notice that she perches crosswise on the branch. Like me. Like Dad.

"You just watch, Gonzo," she says. "You'll be feasting soon."

"Watch what, cheeken-hunter?"

"The river."

Peevo seems over-the-top nice to Gonzo. Some of my buried fears about her grab my guts again. I zoom up to Willo. "Why is she sucking up to him like that?" I ask.

"Wouldn't you if someone threatened to peck your eyes out?"

"Yeah, but don't you get that she's up to something?"

"No, actually."

I'm convinced Peevo's got Willo under some kind of spell. Even me—when I get near her, I get this anxious feeling. My brain goes mushy. Can't think straight. Must be that sweetgrass thing.

Stay clear of her, Wisp.

Just as the setting sun pricks the horizon, it starts.

The river surface starts jiggling.

"There!" Peevo exclaims. "Go get 'em Gonzo! *¡Ándale!*"

Gonzo doesn't budge. "Uh, *perdon?*"

"Minnows, Gonzo. Millions of minnows. They eat the water bugs. You eat the fish. Got it?"

"Of course, but—"

"Not hungry?"

Gonzo erects his white eyebrows and snaps his bill. "I could eat ten cheeken-hawks like you!"

"Too bony," Peevo says. "Follow me."

Gonzo watches dumbstruck as she swoops down to the river.

Peevo drops to within a feather-width of the water and carefully opens her beak.

"Is she, like, eating *fish?*" asks Willo as we fly along above her.

"I wouldn't put it past this freak," I say. "I've seen barn swallows do this. Never tried it myself. Swimming's not my thing."

Peevo skims the surface, expertly scooping up whirligig beetles and water striders.

I fix on her graceful flight, her buffy breast and throat patch, her gilded wingbars that don't scare me like they used to.

"Your turn!" Peevo shouts to Gonzo.

"You theenk I eat lousy bugs?"

"Works for fish, too," Peevo says. "Just open your beak and they'll hop right in."

"*¡Ay caramba!*" Gonzo mutters as he drops from the tree.

He starts off okay, skimming so close to the water that each stroke of his wings dimples the surface. Then he opens his beak.

Ker-plop!

Gonzo spins tail-over-beak and lands flat on his back. After much spluttering and Spanish cursing, he shoots out of the water, straight for Peevo.

"Bravo!" says Peevo who dodges his attack at the last second. "Don't open so wide next time. Just the tip of your lower beak."

"You are crazy if you theenk I am—"

"A fish-eater?" Peevo says innocently. "Perhaps I was wrong about your white-feathered clan."

"Of course, you were!" shouts Gonzo. "I mean, you *weren't!* I mean ... forget it!"

Gonzo shakes a halo of water from his feathers and tries again. And again. And again.

Four swims later he gets the hang of it. First one minnow. Then three. Then scores of minnows down the hatch.

A trio of buffleheads, two males and a female, almost crashes into Gonzo as they chase each other downstream. A flock of mallards circles over the river as if baffled by the sight of a fishing raven. A dozen Arctic terns, their silvery wings dazzling in the day's last sunshine, swoop down beside Gonzo, hunting the same minnows in much the same way.

"You see," he says proudly, as he returns to his high perch above the river. "Feesh have good reason to fear me!"

"I do see," Peevo says, as the four of us well-fed birds settle in for our first night in the Boreal Forest.

It must have been those Arctic terns, fishing beside Gonzo. They flew straight into my dream.

I'm flying high above a thin cloud. At first, I think I'm back in the Andes, but I see no peaks poking through. No birds, either. I can hear them, though. Other nighthawks far behind me. I can't tell how many. Lots, I think. I'm itching to know what lies below the cloud. But not yet. Somehow I know I should wait to find just the right place to pop through.

I close my dream eyes and focus on that spot in the front of my skull where my inner navigator looks out at the world. I get that feeling again, like a thin stream of cool air is connecting to that spot, pulling me forward. This force is stronger than ever, yet it feels kind of ... welcoming, like I could just fold my wings and let it pull me along to its source. What's really weird is that, for the first time, I can actually *see* the flyway in front of me. It looks like a long, glowing branch. I follow it as it bends down through a hole in the cloud and I shoot straight through.

I hear waves crashing. I see thousands of birds with silvery wings. They skim above the dark blue water of a Tundra lake. Like the glowing flyway that pulls me out of the sky, all their flight paths lead to a giant raven, standing in the middle of the lake. Its terrible black wings seem to stretch to both horizons.

I wake to the spring fever of singing birds. With my eyes still closed, I recognize the tunes of my first neighbors and feel like a hatchling again. Warblers, sparrows, thrushes. Kinglets, grosbeaks, flycatchers. All these different birds have claimed their territory. Everybody's paired up with a mate. Their nests are feathered. Their eggs will be laid any day now.

All these birds are home.

That new itch grabs me again. The achy itch for companionship.

It gets so bad, I start wondering if I could be happy out there alone. On the Tundra, I mean.

My nostrils twitch to the scent of sweetgrass.

I feel feathers ruffling on my back. My sister sometimes uses me as a pillow. I open my eyes. "Time to boogie, Willo."

A soft sigh and more ruffling.

I look over my shoulder and gasp.

Peevo is drooped over my back, fast asleep. "AAGH!"

With a quick flick of my butt, I tip her over and plunge

from the branch. I spot Willo chasing dragonflies over the river.

"Hey, what's the big idea?" I say, like it's all her fault a Guardian was sleeping on top of me.

"What?"

"Taking off on me like that!"

"I couldn't sleep through Gonzo's snoring. Besides, you and Peevo seemed pretty cozy. I didn't want to distur—"

"Get *real!* That freak?"

Willo giggles and shoots after a pair of mating damselflies.

"Willo!"

"Who-hah! Who-hah!" Gonzo zooms toward me. He flies low over the water with his beak open like a super-sized barn swallow. "Hey, Weemp, I figured out a way to catch these feesh even when they're not jumping. All you do is—"

"Great, Gonzo," I say. "So let's get out of here before Bigfoot wakes up."

Willo points a wing to the sky. "Too late," she says. "Good morning, Peevo!"

"Well, aren't you little Miss Sunshine," I grumble as Peevo circles above us.

"Aw, Wisp. She's okay. Like, she could have been thrown in the Hutch for teaching me Spanish."

"Yeah, right," I say. "She's probably signaling her squadron as we speak."

"You're paranoid."

"You're a sucker."

"Hey, guys," Peevo says.

I roll my eyes at Willo. *"Hey, guys."*

"Now that we've fueled up," Peevo says, "I think maybe we should leave the river."

"I theenk maybe no," Gonzo says.

"But, Peevo," Willo says. "We just got here! And you said the Athabasca flows pretty much due north. So, why leave it?"

"Well, it's not really the way we want to go."

I'd forgotten how fast Peevo can piss me off. "Not the way *you* want to go, maybe. *We* are following the river. Come on, Willo."

"I'm weeth you, Weemp," Gonzo says, taking another false charge at Peevo. "The feesh are calling my name!"

"Have it your way," Peevo says. "But there's a lot of nasty human stuff downstream that you don't want to—"

"Hey, remember I was hatched on top of a school!" I shout. "I can handle a few humans." My mind flips back to the humans we saw hacking away at the burnt-out rainforest. *Could it get nastier than that?*

"Okay," says Peevo, falling back into her tailing mode. "But whatever you see, whatever you do, keep flying. Don't stop."

I get a whiff of what Peevo means a few thousand wingbeats downstream.

29

INTO THE MESS
Alberta Tar Sands

"Eeew!" Willo says. "What's that stink?"

I had tried to ignore it. I'd hoped the Athabasca's green glory would go on and on, deep into the Boreal Forest.

I'd wanted to prove Peevo dead wrong.

But now there's no denying it. Something foul is in the air. Even I can smell it.

"I theenk a lot of humans farted all at once," Gonzo says.

I'd seen it coming. Peevo's nasty human stuff. First, it was a bunch of long, skinny lines of mowed-down trees. Next came huge blobs of forest, stripped naked down to mud, as if the trees had uprooted and run away. Now it's a stinky yellow haze in the air.

Willo flies so close to me I can barely get a flap in edgewise. "I'm getting this freaky feeling," she says.

"Uh-huh," I say. "Humans are good at stinking things up. Get over it."

"No, I mean *that* smell. It reminds me of something."

"What?"

"Don't know."

I take a reluctant sniff. And another. Distant memories pop into my brain. Soft brood feathers tickling my beak. The friendly swish of poplar leaves. The sound of big wide wings. My mother's scream. "I got it."

"Well?"

"Remember how Winnie got stuck in—"

"Hot tar!"

"Yep. That's what you're smelling."

"Awful stuff."

Whuhh-whuhh-whuhh-whuhh-whuhh.

That sound still sends shivers through my wings, especially now, thinking about how my brother died.

"I sure hope that thees is *not* the Tundra," Gonzo says as he flaps up beside us. "No trees is one thing. But no life? Everything suddenly went dark. Besides a few humans and some buzzy stuff from their funny towers and trucks, I am picking up no *luz de vida* at all. *Nada!* Tell me what ees going on down there."

"Welcome to the Tar Sands," says Peevo, who, once again, has silently snuck up beside us.

Stealth flying. A trick known only to owls and Guardian nighthawks. As much as I'd like to learn it, I'd never ask her.

I ignore Peevo, riveted by the gross scene below.

The four of us fly side by side over a railway line that marks the boundary between the living and the dead. Bright green poplar stands and beaver ponds give way to oily muck. The songs of birds are replaced by the groan of machines. The land itself is steaming, just like Yellowstone.

"Diss-gusting," Willo says. "What's up with this?"

"Human feeding frenzy," Peevo says.

"They eat *tar*?" Willo says.

Peevo chuckles. "Their machines do. Humans scrape and squeeze the ground to make food for all their machines."

I hate how Peevo has an answer for everything, how she knows so much about the world. And only a year older than me.

I instinctively reach for height as the air gets hotter, stinkier.

Meanwhile Gonzo is plunging into the mess.

He's used to bad smells. "Uh, Gonzo," I call. "Where are you going?"

"I can sense some water down there."

"You don't want to go there, Gonzo," Peevo says.

"You don't know nutheeng, cheeken-hunter. Where there's water, there's feesh!"

"It's a stretch to even *call* that water!" Peevo shouts after him.

As usual, Gonzo has his own ideas. He pulls his wings into a half-tuck and swoops towards a huge pond that's covered in a scum of rainbow-colored oil.

I plunge after him, thinking, one gulp of that icky stuff or a splash of it on his wings and Gonzo's a dead duck. Down in Texas last fall, I'd seen lots of ducks floating belly-up in an equally disgusting pond.

"Stay high, Willo!" I cry without looking back. "Get way up there! Don't follow me!"

"Aww!" she whines.

"Forget it, Gonzo!" I yell. "You can fish once we get out of this mess!"

"Too bad you don't like feesh!" Gonzo yells back, now going into a full tuck.

I know I can beat Gonzo on a dead-drop dive. I did it over Popocatépetl volcano and I can do it again.

But Gonzo has a huge head start this time.

"Gonzo, STOP!"

"Get off my back, Weemp. I'm hungry for feesh!"

I barely hear him through the roar of wind past my ears. The stench of oil and tar and smoke floods my nostrils.

Gonzo levels off just above the oil slick.

I take aim, tuck myself into a spear-point, and hurtle toward him.

Gonzo opens his beak just as I streak to his side.

"DON'T!" I yell.

BOOM!

A deafening crack batters my skull. One wingtip grazes the surface of the oil slick. I flare my wings to shake off the oil. My tail feathers break the surface and get coated in more gunk.

"Gonzo! Help!"

I madly flap to keep airborne.

Whuhh-whuhh-whuhh-whuhh-whuhh.

Gonzo circles back and zooms straight for me, a flash of panic in his eyes.

He thrusts out his legs. He splays his dinosaur feet.

Not again.

The impact knocks the wind out of me.

BOOM!

I feel Gonzo lurch at the sound of another crack. Now,

locked together, we're both nose-diving toward the gunk.

I can only groan.

Gonzo pumps the air like a mad eagle, straining for lift. He catches some air with less than a feather to spare before we would have hit the surface of that killer pond.

BOOM!

"*¡Ay caramba!*" Gonzo says, even as he lifts me high above the Tar Sands. "Thees is one freekin' crazy place!"

BOOM!

"Uh ... thanks, Gonzo," I say when I can breathe again. "Could you maybe let me go?"

"But you got all that steenky stuff on your feathers."

"No, really. Let me try. If I fall, would you mind catching me again?"

"If you inseest."

"But let's not make this a habit, okay?"

"Okay, but you are not the first cheeken-hawk I catch, eef you know what I mean."

"I get you, Gonzo."

I feel a slight tremor come through Gonzo's feet, like he's just realized how close we both came to biting it. He lets go.

"Ouch!" I cry as I catch a wing on Gonzo's claws.

I can barely flap my soiled wing. The other one burns where Gonzo hooked me. And my steering is all wonky, thanks to an oily tail.

But I'm airborne.

I'm alive.

"*Gracias*, Gonzo," I say as we spiral up together.

"*De nada, amigo.* I ... how you say ... owed you one."

We climb high above the Tar Sands until I can see the

Boreal Forest pick up again far to the north. I was beginning to wonder if this dead zone went on forever.

"What was that *loco* sound?" Gonzo asks as we level off at five thousand wingbeats.

"I think it's supposed to scare off birds," I say.

"I theenk maybe it worked."

I laugh as I casually start looking around for Willo.

Nothing but yellow haze.

"Are you picking up any life forms, Gonzo? Like, my sister?"

Gonzo swings into a wide circle. He opens his beak and slowly rocks it left and right, up and down, scanning the whole sky. "Nobody but us cheekens, Weemp."

"Very funny."

That's when it hits me. Deep in my gizzard. In the flurry to save Gonzo, I'd left my sister in the clutches of a wily Guardian who I trust about as much as Flare himself.

Zero.

30

STEERING HOME
Slave River, Northwest Territories

"Stop scaring me like that," I say.

"I didn't mean to," Willo says.

"Where have I heard that line before?"

"Uh ... Peevo?"

"You're even beginning to sound like her."

I hear muffled giggling beside Willo.

Our uninvited Guardian guest is trying hard to be one of the gang since our disgusting day at the Tar Sands. After much frantic sky searching, Gonzo and I had finally spotted Willo eight thousand wingbeats above that stinking wasteland. Peevo explained that the yellow haze burned Willo's eyes, so she thought it best to rise above it and get some fresh air.

Yeah, right.

Peevo has been acting extra protective of Willo these days, like an older sister or a second mom. Warning her of sudden downdrafts, fussing over where Willo should sleep, sharing the fattest bugs with her. I hear them talking Spanish sometimes. Once, when they were blabbing away about *loco* this and *canario* that, they started laughing so hard they almost fell out of the sky. I thought of asking Gonzo to translate but was too proud to ask.

To add to my misery, Peevo has been teaching Willo some flying tricks that even *I* don't know. Like low-level stealth flying and doing a backward somersault while hovering.

Make me sick.

I fly above the Slave River valley in grumpy silence.

I eventually lose myself in Boreal beauty. I notice that the late May leaves are a lot smaller this far north. Big pans of rotten ice still drift down the river. Flock after flock of ducks, geese, and swans quack, honk, and trumpet all around us. I realize we're all moving north on the cutting edge of spring.

This begins to worry me. *Will the Tundra still be frozen when I get there?*

A hundred Arctic terns explode off a mudflat as our shadows streak over them and I find myself thinking of the silver-winged birds of my crazy dream. My dream of a giant raven, who lives on a Tundra lake and has wings as wide as this valley.

This strange image, which both frightens and fascinates me, reminds me that, as much as I love the Boreal Forest, I can't stop now, not here. With each wing-flap, I can feel the call of the Tundra getting stronger. But honestly, I don't know what to make of it anymore. I can thank

Peevo for totally confusing me on this. *Others will follow you, Wisp.*

What the heck does that mean?

All I know is that each day I must fly due north, farther and faster than the day before.

And my strange flock is beginning to grumble.

"What's the big rush?" Willo whines. "The Tundra, *if* it exists, is probably still covered in snow."

She's thinking that, too.

"Snow?" Gonzo says. "What ees that?"

"You've never seen it?" Willo asks.

Gonzo shakes his head. "*Nunca,* never."

"It's this crusty white stuff that can freeze your feet."

"Oh, *nieve.* I have heard about thees. Only in mountains, no?"

"Uh, no, Gonzo," I say. "Might be a little bit on the Tundra."

Gonzo makes an upside-down lunge at me. "You deed not tell me thees, Weemp."

"Don't worry, Gonzo," I say. "The caribou will be there with or without snow."

"This Yellowlife place, ees there—"

"It's, uh, Yellow*knife,* Gonzo."

"*Exactamente.* Is there any snow there now?"

"No, Gonzo. But—"

"So why not we stop there to go feeshing? Maybe feesh the dumpsters, too, no?"

"You're addicted, Gonzo."

"Yeah," Willo cries. "Why not stop there?"

I huff and pull way ahead of the flock.

I feel a cracking inside.

Two bearings come out of hiding and start battling inside

of me. Go *northwest*, take a side trip to my nesting place in Yellowknife. Or go *due north* to the Tundra, where my inner navigator is pulling me.

This battle gets fiercer, the closer I get to Moosehead School.

I shake my head, trying to silence the war within.

It only gets louder.

I'm through with Yellowknife. What's the thrill in claiming old turf? Any bird can do that. Half of it burned down, anyway. I'm out to find a new home, claim new territory. To live free, wherever and however I like. Arctic Tundra, here we come!

I pump my wings harder yet, aiming due north, knowing that I've made up my mind, once and for all.

Then again ... what's the harm in just one teeny look at the place where I hatched? Maybe let's visit it on the way to the Tundra. Just a little detour, right?

My brain turns to pulp. My beak aches from clenching it. I feel ripped in two.

Until Peevo barges in.

"I'm with you on this one, Wisp," she says. "Let's push north to the Tundra. You don't want to stop in Yellowknife."

That settles it! My swollen pride and bruised ego kick all logic and reason, hopes and dreams, right out of my head. My inner battle becomes an outer battle.

Between Peevo and me.

I slam on the airbrakes until I'm beak-to-beak with Peevo. "How would *you* know what *I* want?" I cut her off and make a sharp turn northwest, straight for Yellowknife. "Come on, Willo, Gonzo. Time for school!"

I close my eyes for a few wingbeats, letting raw instinct steer me back to my first and only real home. I totally ignore the shrieking of my inner navigator, now more powerful than ever, calling me to an entirely different destination.

31

NO TURNING BACK

Great Slave Lake, Northwest Territories

I suddenly feel more bite to my wings. The air here is colder, denser. I look ahead and see the rocky shore of Great Slave Lake. Thick pans of candle ice bob in the cold, clear water. A big spruce tree leans over the lake, aiming a long, knobby shadow directly at Yellowknife Bay.

I can't believe we've flown so far. From Ecuador to Yellowknife. Almost.

As we lift high above the lake, Willo doesn't need my nagging to pick up the pace. She's cruising right beside me, and I'm actually working hard to keep up.

Peevo, however, is less than thrilled to see Great Slave. That suits me just fine. Says I'm still in control here.

"Listen ... uh ... Wisp," she calls, "I really think we should skip the—"

"Who's *we*?" I shout without looking back.

"Okay, us, you, whoever."

"Look, Bigfoot, I planned this trip for one bird. That would be *me*. I count three freeloaders."

"I said you would find followers," Peevo says.

"When I'm not even looking?"

"That's the way it works sometimes."

"Give me a break!"

"Really, Wisp," Peevo says. "I think we ought to, I mean, *you* ought to—"

"To what? Pack it in after flying all this way? Go back to the Refugium with my tail between my legs and surrender to your goon-faced buddies?"

"No, no, I mean, I just think you're cruising for trouble if you—"

"Look!" cries Willo. "Yellowknife!" She is first to spot the orange cap of the town's mining headframe.

The sight of it gets my heart pounding. Standing three hundred wingbeats high, this is the tallest human structure in the Boreal Forest and a magnet for any birds passing this way.

Any, that is, but Peevo. The closer we get, the antsier she gets. "Can you talk to him?" I hear her say to Willo. "Maybe convince him to detour around Yellowknife. Like, *way* around?"

"Why, Peevo?" I jump in. "I mean, what exactly *is* your problem?"

"In a word, Flare."

Acid pours into my stomach. A tiny troubling thought worms into my brain and explodes. *Have I put winning a fight with Peevo ahead of avoiding a fight with Flare?* I stare hard at Peevo who circles below me. "Are you leading us into a trap?" I shout.

"Out of one, actually," Peevo says. "At least, I tried to."

"So what's he planning?"

"Don't have a clue."

"You really don't know *anything*?"

"Like I said, I haven't seen Flare's squadron since Panama. What I do know is this: Flare's no dummy."

"No?"

"Well, okay, sure he is. But what he lacks in brainpower he makes up in willpower. If Flare wants something, he won't rest till he gets it. He's unstoppable, Wisp. And he wants you *real bad*."

"But we ditched him, didn't we?" Willo asks.

"You did. Congratulations. But so what? He didn't need to track you. Join the dots, Wisp. However much you zigzagged, all your flight paths ultimately pointed to Yellowknife. Even Flare could figure that out. He knew the pull would be irresistible."

I could've resisted it. I could still. I can skip Yellowknife and go straight to the Tundra.

But I'm lying to myself. I realize that, this close to the nest, raw instinct rules.

Irresistible.

I lock my eyes on the headframe as it sucks me across the lake. The mere sight of it stifles any lingering dread or doubt I may have about coming here. My whole body catches fire with one thought. *I'm home!*

I climb and climb above Great Slave Lake until the rest of my little flock is a quivering blur against the ice pans. I carve wide circles over them, randomly darting like a swallow, hovering like a tern, soaring like a hawk.

Just like Dad.

I can barely contain this energy.

Then it starts. A spine-tingling call that, for the first time in my life, erupts from deep in my throat.

Beerb ... Beerb ... Beerb ... Beerb.

After a slow, silent stall, I pull in my wings and drop into a tailspin, spiraling straight for ... Peevo.

I blur past her, grazing a wing. Seconds before almost crashing into the lake, I thrust my wings forward, spread my tail feathers and get them screaming.

V-R-R-R-O-O-O-O-M!

I end my show with an inside loop, break into a full barrel-roll, and smoothly click back into place a couple of beak-lengths ahead of Gonzo.

"*¡Loco chotocabra!*"

As much as I love doing tricks with Gonzo, I know this act is mine alone. "Can't help it, Gonzo," I say, doing my best to sound sane.

The fever passes for a few wingbeats but soon heats up again. Just as I angle my wings to climb, Willo and Peevo start circling around me.

"Uh ... look, Wisp," Willo says, "Don't you think you're a little exposed up there? I mean who's not going to see you showing off?"

"Or *hear* you?" Peevo adds.

But it's too late. The fever engulfs me again and I'm pumping into another steep climb.

32

HEADFRAME

Yellowknife Bay, Northwest Territories

In spite of all my frosty talk and crazy air shows, I'm secretly glad to tuck in closer with my strange flock as we cruise toward the bald north shore of Great Slave Lake.

Yellowknife is not exactly what I'd been aiming for all along but, for the moment, it feels right. Very right. After billions of wingbeats, the storm of restlessness that whisked me all the way from the Amazon seems spent.

Tamed, at least.

Meanwhile, my brain is still dulled by the fever of coming home. Flare is the furthest thing from my mind.

I instinctively pull up and veer away from shore when I spot a big brown and white raptor leap from a lakeside pine. I study it gliding above the water, wings swept back in two trim v's.

That wing shape. I remember now. Osprey. Fish-eater. Harmless.

I veer back and follow it just a hundred wingbeats up.

"Hey, Weemp, what are you doing?" Gonzo cries.

"Watch this," I say. "Right below us."

Gonzo opens his beak, tips it to the lake, and rocks it back and forth.

The osprey swoops low to the water, slows almost to a stall, hovers, then—*SPLOOSH*—it plunges in with open talons.

"There's a trick for you!" I say.

"Forget it."

"No, wait."

The four of us circle the spot where the osprey disappeared.

A big spray of water and up it comes with a pearly trout in its claws. It shoots out of the lake, pauses in midair to shake off the water, and slings the fish away to its nest.

It's been so long.

It feels so good.

To be home.

The giant orange-topped headframe pulls me into Yellowknife. The others follow, our flock tighter than ever. The headframe is so tall I have to climb steeply to land on its flat metal roof.

Bad move.

I don't see who's waiting for us up top.

A ring of ravens descends on us in a cloud of glistening black feathers.

"*Keer-uck! Keer-uck!*" go the ravens as they pounce, pinning us with their feet. "Took you long enough," says the biggest one who wears a beard of long, scruffy feathers and a thatch of fuzz on his belly that covers his legs like trousers.

"Been watching you, like, *all day*. It's long past suppertime!"

My lungs shrink and I have to gasp for air. *Not this again.* Memories of Gonzo's bloodthirsty beach bums fill my head. "Say something, Gonzo," I squeak.

"What's that, runt-hawk?" growls the bearded raven. He snaps his beak. He pops his jaws.

"Uh ... nothing. I just wanted to introduce my friend here." I jab Gonzo in the gut.

Gonzo bows low, flaring his tail and wings.

I notice that Gonzo is about a third bigger than all the other ravens. Trouble is, there's only one of him and hundreds of them.

Gonzo clears his throat. *"Buenos dias, amigos."*

The bearded raven inflates his neck and vibrates his hackles. A chorus of high-pitched trilling erupts from the circle of ravens around him.

This is not good.

It's Willo's turn to jab Gonzo. "These guys wouldn't know Spanish, stupid," she whispers.

"Stupid?" roars the bearded raven, towering over Willo.

More bill snapping all around. The trilling noise swells, slicing into my brain. I can't move. Can't talk.

Gonzo stands to his full height. His white eye tufts pop out of his head. A ring of white spears springs from his neck.

Uh-oh. That's really going to piss them off.

But no. Gonzo's display has a totally different impact.

The bearded raven jumps off Gonzo's toes. The other ravens back away to the edge of the headframe.

"Uh, what's up with the feathers?" the bearded raven says slowly.

"Feathers?" Gonzo says.

"The ... the *white* ones."

Gonzo spreads his shoulders. He points his beak to the sky. "I am from the white-feathered clan of feesh-eaters."

I have to choke back a laugh. *Go get 'em, Gonzo!*

A hush falls over the ravens. The bearded one squints at Gonzo. "Fish-eaters?"

Gonzo grandly sweeps a wing toward Yellowknife Bay. He cocks his head to the sparkling waters far below. "Even now I can hear the feesh calling my name. Gonzo ... Gonzo ... offering themselves to me!"

What a ham.

"Where do you come from?" asks the bearded raven.

"I come from the faraway land of Panama."

"You mean, you flew all that way? You ... *migrated*?"

"Of course. What ees there to fear in crossing two continents?"

"But ... ravens don't do that."

"No? Who says?"

"But—"

"You should try it sometime. There are many fresh, juicy, meaty theengs to eat along thee way."

The bearded raven snaps his beak. "We are a hungry flock."

They sure do look scrawny.

"Ravens are always hungry, no?" asks Gonzo.

The bearded raven shakes his head. "Not hungry like us. The humans closed the dump on us. Added big nets, dogs, cannons, guns. Without the dump, this scrubby land can't feed us all."

Gonzo makes an impressive *tsk-tsk-tsk* sound, like he's about to cry.

I force a grin into a grimace, like I'm really hurting for these guys.

"What about dumpsters?" Gonzo asks.

"All locked up now."

"Then what about all thee careeboo?"

"Winter, sure. Some trickle through here. But now, they're all out on the Tundra."

Gonzo glances at me and winks.

Finally he believes me.

"Okay," says Gonzo. "So, eat careeboo in weenter, feesh in summer, no?"

The bearded raven lowers his head.

Gonzo scrunches up his beak. "You mean ... you *don't* catch feesh?"

"That's for ospreys and eagles, not—"

"And *smart* ravens like you!" Gonzo says.

The bearded raven snaps out of Gonzo's spell. He steps back on Gonzo's toes. "You're bluffing. Why go for fish when we can eat you?"

The other ravens inch forward. They start that terrible trilling again.

Gonzo flashes his brilliant eyelids at his captor. "You eat us, and you get one lousy meal. Let me teach you how to feesh, and you weel never go hungry again, *amigo.* You have my promeese."

The bearded raven locks his eyes on me. "And your puny friends?"

"The *chotocabras*, I mean ... how you say ... nighthawks, they are my teaching asseestants. You need them, too." Gonzo gives his wings a quick flip. "So, deal or no deal?"

The bearded raven hops from foot to foot. He bobs

his head. He turns to look at the circle of starving ravens around him.

Gonzo stretches his amazing wings. "Come on, let's go. I'll show you how to feesh."

I hold my breath.

All the ravens cock their heads at their bearded leader, who gradually backs out of Gonzo's face. "All right, then," he says. "Show us."

"Yesss!" I say, pumping one wing.

Gonzo struts victoriously to the edge of the headframe.

In the sweet relief of the moment, my fever breaks and my head clears. I look out to the Yellowknife skyline as if seeing it for the first time. *What am I doing here? What happened to my Tundra adventure? Have I thrown my dream away just like poor old Tamas? And where's Flare? Have I stupidly led us into his trap?*

I stare at Gonzo. He might just save us from these bloodthirsty ravens. Maybe he can protect us from Flare, too, *if* he shows up. Maybe even save my dream.

A plan pops into my head.

Gonzo lifts his wings, ready to drop over the edge.

"*Wait!*" I cry. All the ravens skewer me with their hungry eyes.

"Yes, rat bird?" croaks the bearded raven.

"I ... uh ... just wanted to give Gonzo some final fishing tips."

Gonzo turns his head and blinks at me.

I give him a pleading look.

Gonzo gets it. "Of course," he says, hopping over to me. "*Con permiso*," he says to the bearded raven. "Please excuse us," and he wraps his huge wing around me in a huddle.

The bearded raven snorts. He rakes the metal roof with his claws.

I whisper my plan to Gonzo.

"Sounds good to me," he says, hopping away with a big show of wings. "Now we will catch even *more* feesh!"

Gonzo struts back to the edge of the headframe, catches a gust, and drops out of sight.

A torrent of black wings follows him.

Willo and I are left alone on the bare headframe roof.

Willo and I.

Willo whips her head around. "Where's Peevo?"

"I thought she was beside you."

"Nope."

My wings go stiff. "I *told* you she was up to something."

"Maybe she, I don't know, saw all the ravens and took off."

"Maybe not."

I scan the evening sky for a lone bird with dagger-shaped wings. Nothing but a few gulls chasing a crow. A floatplane lifting off above some houseboats. I search the skyline of stubby office towers and leaning shacks. The charred hulks of houses torched in last summer's fire still blanket the edge of town. I spot a green and yellow building shaped a bit like a frog.

Moosehead Public School.

"It survived the fire," I say under my breath.

"Great, but don't you think we should find Peevo before we—"

I can hardly hear her. The fever has recaptured my brain. Without giving Peevo or Flare another thought, I plunge over the side and zoom straight for the place where I was hatched.

33

AMBUSH

Moosehead School, Yellowknife, Northwest Territories

The school roof is exactly as I remembered. It triggers a mishmash of memories. Snuggling under Mom's breast. Fighting with my siblings. Listening to Dad's stories. Thrilling to his aerobatic stunts. Discovering I'd never be the Navigator he wanted me to be. Freaking out after the fire split our family apart.

There's no sign of Flare but I'm getting antsy to flee.

"Look at this!" Willo exclaims, pointing to an exposed patch of tar. "You can still see Winnie's tracks."

I shoot another look at the sky and hop over to her. "And this," I say, staring at Dad's frantic wingprints made just before a raven plucked our brother off the roof.

My heart jumps to a sharp click behind us. I turn to where

the sound came from—a tall metal box at the edge of the roof. I'd never noticed it before.

"Freeze," I whisper to Willo.

Though we could easily fly away, I don't budge. I have to know what made that sound. I only hope we're invisible against the gray-brown pebbles.

The box cracks open, revealing a door. In the dusky light, I can just make out a human hand. It slowly pushes against the door and out steps a boy.

My first instinct is to bolt since he reminds me right away of the boy who chucked rocks at us down in Puebla. He's about the same size, even has the same dark hair and eyes. But I sense by the way he moves that he won't hurt us.

The boy stands totally silent and still for a few moments, staring wide-eyed at us. Then he looks up at the sky, tightens his mouth, and makes a life-saving sound that Willo and I have passed back and forth many times since leaving the Amazon. *"Queek-queek! Queek-queek!"*

A nighthawk alarm call.

"Do you believe it?" Willo whispers. "A *human* calling like that?"

"Shh. Listen."

At the outer limits of my hearing, I detect a faraway response.

"Queek-queek! Queek-queek!"

The boy lifts something with two glassy eyes to his face.

"Who's he looking at?" whispers Willo.

"Dunno."

"Peevo?"

"Would you shush," I say. "Guardians don't *do* alarm calls."

What I hear next raises my nape feathers so fast they almost pop off.

Beerb ... Beerb ... Beerb.

Willo beats her wings against her back. "*Queek-queek! Queek-queek!*" she calls at the top of her lungs.

I bat her down with one wing. "What are you doing? It could be a trick!"

The boy whips out a small square box and holds it to his face.

"But listen, Wisp!" Willo says right out loud. "It's *got* to be!"

Beerb ... Beerb ... Beerb.

I can't believe my ears. I can't trust my heart. "No, Willo. It's a trap! Let's get out of here!"

The boy points his little box at us.

I tense my wings for takeoff.

A flash of light blinds me.

Beerb ... Beerb ... Beerb.

When my sight returns, I look up to see the blurred silhouette of a lone nighthawk shooting toward us. Before I can lift a wing, the nighthawk is right on us, shaking the pebbles loose with his boom.

V-R-R-R-O-O-O-O-M!

Another flash of light.

I can't see a thing.

"Wisp!" comes a voice I thought I'd never hear again. "Willo!"

I blink away the blindness.

Then tears get in the way.

I open my eyes to the beaming face of my father.

Damon traps us in a wing-hug that I hope will never end.

FLASH!

"Dad! Dad! Dad!" Willo keeps saying. "We thought you—"

"Not now, Willo. We have to—"

I jerk my head above the tangle of wings. Below all the laughing and sniffling and rustling of feathers, I hear a deep rumble.

"Dad," I whisper. "Listen."

The three of us lift our beaks to the sky.

The door behind us clicks shut.

My pounding heart is drowned out by the rush of Guardian wings.

34

THE SCARIEST BIRD EVER

Moosehead School, Yellowknife, Northwest Territories

"Hmm," grunts Flare. "Quite a catch! More than I'd bargained for."

This time the squadron leader has taken no chances. Ten burly Guardians stand wing-to-wing in a tight snare around us. Another ten form a whirling airborne net above us.

Willo, Dad, and I form a ball of wings in the middle.

"I'd forgotten how very *small* you are, Wisp," Flare says, spitting out my name like yesterday's vomit. "And how very *stupid*."

"Likewise," I say as a creeping nausea invades every cell of my body.

Standing by Flare's side, coming up only to his shoulder, is the littlest Guardian and, as far as I'm concerned, the biggest rat alive.

"Mind if we join you for a bit?" Peevo asks.

"Anyone but you," I hiss.

Flare props his wings on his belly like a mother hen. He huffs dramatically, flooding my lungs with his skunky breath. "What? You two got into a little tiff?"

"She's even more horrible than *you*!" Willo cries.

Never trust a Guardian, eh, Willo?

Damon hops in front of us with wings spread. "Please, Flare, let them go. You can take me wherever you like."

"I'll hear none of that, *vagrant-breeder*! I wouldn't think of separating your lovely family. You know, I'm a big believer in togetherness. I think it's much nicer to travel together, to sightsee together, to be *thrown in the Hutch together*! Don't you agree?"

Flare leans back and starts gently clapping his wingtips in front of his feathered paunch. "I've decided that instead of bringing all this to a flying finish here and now, I would rather make the *most of your misery*, by escorting you back to the home you've been longing for. Right, Guardians?"

His squadron responds in one terrible voice. "Hutch! Hutch! Hutch! *Hutch! Hutch!*"

All but Peevo join in. She just stares at me, looking seriously anxious.

Is she trying to tell me something?

I hear the door behind us swing open again. Now there are two voices, the boy's and a man's, both sounding super-excited.

FLASH!

Flare raises a wing before his eyes. A ripple of alarm goes through the Guardians. They shuffle on their fat feet.

I'd forgotten how much Guardians fear humans.

Peevo doesn't take her eyes off me.

FLASH!

"Close your eyes," Damon whispers. "Don't look at the light. This could go on for a bit."

"How do you know, Dad?" I whisper back.

"I couldn't fly after that water bomber knocked me off the roof. Even with all the fire and explosions and screaming, that man stopped to pick me up off the road. He kept me in the school to look after my broken wing."

"All winter?" I say.

Damon nods. "He and his son are real bird lovers. Always pointing that flashbox thing at me. It's harmless."

Flare bats Damon over the head. "Shut up, Plebe!"

I flinch like I took the hit.

FLASH!

With each burst of light, the Guardians get twitchier.

Flare gets madder. "Squadron, smarten up! Hold your formations! What are ya, chicks?"

FLASH!

Willo presses her head against my back. I burrow against my father's chest, clinging to his scent.

FLASH-FLASH!

The boy and the man get more excited, chattering and pointing.

More shuffling of Guardian feet. Nervous muttering from the airborne troops.

"What do you think you're doing?" Flare yells. "Maintain formation! Stick together. Together! That's an order!"

FLASH!

I lift my head and peek at Flare's mighty squadron. They're beginning to scatter like scaredy-cat chickens.

"*Togetherness*, eh, Flare?"

Flare's eyes spit fire. He leaps into the air and comes crashing down on the three of us. He flattens Dad and Willo against the roof while clamping his well-clawed feet around my throat.

FLASH!

"Uh ... just kidding," I splutter.

"I won't let you slip through my claws this time, you stinking dung beetle!"

FLASH!

Flare steps on my head and grinds my beak into the roof. I try to struggle free, sending a spray of pebbles in his face. He presses harder and I think I hear a cracking sound in my skull. I have to work at every breath. I'm about to black out when I feel a loosening of his grip. Through one eye, half-covered by his fat foot, I see him straighten up and shout at his squadron, now in shambles. "Come back here, you cowards! It's just some harmless human trick."

FLASH!

I feel hot breath by my ear. For an instant, Peevo's sweetgrass scent cuts through Flare's stupefying stink.

"Whatever happens," Peevo whispers, "whatever you see, don't leave the roof till I tell you. Just *don't*."

Before I can even try to wrench my head around, Peevo is gone.

What is she up to now?

Flare suddenly eases up on his death grip.

I get my beak back. I can breathe again.

All shuffling stops.

I look up and over Flare's shoulder to see his airborne net disintegrate.

FLASH-FLASH!

The human chatter rises to a fever pitch.

Flare hops right off us and stares up at the sky. "What in dirt's name?" he mutters.

What's left of his squadron is dumbly staring in the same direction.

FLASH-FLASH-FLASH!

Except for Peevo. She's staring right at me, secretly tapping one wing on the pebbles.

Don't leave the roof till I tell you.

I stare back at her, torn apart by one question that could change my life forever. *Do I trust her this time?*

A flash from Peevo's pleading eyes, almost as bright as from the human's little box, clinches my decision.

That wasn't fake.

Gonzo and I had a plan for this kind of trouble. But I don't flee. I wait for her sign. All I can trust at this point is that burning look I saw in her eyes.

I gesture for Dad and Willo to stay put. They both shrug but do as I say. We slowly stand and turn to see what's up.

I blink hard.

Sculling slowly toward us from the shore of Yellowknife Bay, is the biggest, blackest, scariest bird *ever*.

Bigger than an airplane.

Blacker than a moonless night.

Scarier than even the giant raven of my dream.

"This can't be happening," Willo whispers.

"Bless the winds," says Damon, pulling us closer yet.

FLASH-FLASH, FLASH-FLASH-FLASH!

The giant bird speaks.

"*Keer-uck! Keer-uck!*" it shrieks with the sound of hundreds of voices.

"A raven?" Willo says.

"Guess so," Damon says, looking at me sideways. "I wonder where it's been hiding."

"The Tundra," Willo says, like she really believes it.

I'd believe it, too, if it hadn't been my idea.

The giant raven shrieks again as it glides overhead. "*Keer-uck! Keer-uck!*"

It stops above the school. It fills the air with a terrible thunder that goes on and on. *Whuhh-whuhh-whuhh-whuhh-whuhh.* Its hovering form ebbs and flows as if underwater.

FLASH-FLASH-FLASH!

Flare's beak falls open. His wings go limp.

Until the rain starts.

The white rain.

It first appears from beneath the giant bird itself. It spreads out and falls like a tattered sheet, sinking slowly, toward the school.

This was not part of the plan.

Pebbles scatter around Flare's shaking feet.

I can hear his beak chattering.

Then, from the very tip of the great bird's beak comes a lone voice. A familiar voice, yet foreign, hailing from a faraway beach in Panama. "*Who-hah! Who-hah!*"

"Nice work, Gonzo," I whisper to myself.

"Now!" Peevo shouts. "Follow me!"

Dad and Willo zoom behind her.

I lift my wings and take one last look at the sheet of white rain, now just a few wing spans from the roof.

"Now!" Peevo shouts again.

I zip after them seconds before it hits the roof with a great splat.

I take the lead from Peevo and steer us in a wide circle around the school—to enjoy the show.

Flare and his goons are dripping with sticky white goo.

My nostrils fill with the foul stench of raven guano.

Flare takes off like a bat out of hell, trailing a cloud of white mist. *Thunk!* He smacks head-first into the poplar branch that hangs over the school.

The last of Flare's goons zoom right past, spraying him with a fresh layer of goo.

Flare picks himself up, emits a chick-like whimper, and limps into the air, pointed straight south.

"Go back to that birdcage where you belong!" I shout after him.

Peevo grins from cheek to cheek. "*Finally*, he's out of our feathers!"

A hint of that old anger resurfaces. "*Our* feathers?"

"Yes, *our* feathers!" she says.

I pull in front of her and hover.

She brakes and hovers just a wing length away.

Impressive, I think. But this is no time to trade flight secrets. "So how come you took off on us at the headframe?"

"I suspected a trap; you knew that. But not from ravens. I saw them just in time to escape. I circled above the headframe, keeping an eye on you, listening in—though I couldn't hear your plan."

Those Guardian ears. Spooky.

"When I saw Gonzo go fishing with the others, it struck me that he might be able to help you if Flare showed up."

"We already had that covered," I say. "But how did you know what was coming? The guano bomb, I mean. That wasn't part of our plan."

Peevo laughs. "Gonzo's idea."

"Nice touch."

"I raced back to the headframe to tell you about it, but you'd gone tearing off to the school. Flare intercepted me before I got there, so I made like I was thrilled to see him and couldn't wait to rejoin the squadron."

"Just in time for our capture."

"I had nothing to do with that. He'd spotted you the moment you started your crazy air show over the lake."

"Just like you said."

"Yep."

Willo and Dad fly over to us. "Come on, you two!" Willo yells.

"We're good to go now," I say. "Follow that bird!"

"I'm in," Dad says.

"*That* bird?" Willo says, looking up at the giant raven as it drifts into the Boreal dusk.

"It's going due north, isn't it?" Peevo says.

I quickly check in with my inner navigator. It's still there, getting stronger. *Gonzo's right on course.* "Sure is," I say. "Could be a really cool vortex behind that bird. We could fly all the way to the Tundra with our eyes closed."

WHERE EXACTLY?

Arctic Tundra, Northwest Territories

"That was a good trick, Gonzo," I say, watching the spruce trees thin out below us.

"The feeshing? Oh, yes, I finally catch one with my feet."

"No, the giant guano bomb."

"Oh, you know I like very much to make treex."

"How did you get everyone to dump their load all at once? You spooked those Guardians right out of their feathers."

"Come on, Weemp," Gonzo says. "What good is a treek if I geev everytheeng away?"

A wave of raven laughter fans out behind us. From *lots* of ravens. The whole hungry headframe mob that pounced on us. *Was that just yesterday?* It seems like such a long time ago.

Gonzo must have made quite a splash with those ravens. Between his beefy Latino build, his weird white feathers, and the fishing lessons, he'd made a few hundred friends in one afternoon. Many wingbeats back, the monster raven had fallen apart, scattering into the rowdy flock of birds that had so much fun creating it. Now they're loosely spread out behind Gonzo and me.

I never asked for this role. I never wanted it. I totally resist it every time Peevo brings it up. This whole leader thing. *How did it come to this?* Me, leading my little sister, my long-lost dad, a Guardian deserter, a blind raven, and a huge mob of his crazy friends to the Tundra.

So much for my solo adventure.

This is turning into something totally different. I don't know what, but it actually feels okay.

"How far are your buddies going?" I ask Gonzo.

"They wanted at least to see the tree line."

"I think we're basically over it."

"Okay, just a leetle farther then. Maybe poke their beaks out onto the Tundra, no?"

"Did you infect them with your migration bug?"

"You know ravens don't ..." Gonzo starts. "Okay, maybe *some* ravens migrate. A leetle beet. But, you know, once I showed these guys how to feesh, there ees no need to worry about closed dump een Yellowknife, no need to dream of careeboo."

"No more *chotocabra* lunches, no?" I say, laying on a thick Gonzo accent.

Peevo chuckles on my other side.

I was positive Peevo was a Flare plant. But she came through in the end. Since leaving Yellowknife, I've felt okay about sharing my personal airspace with her. Very okay. Occasionally she'll inch ahead of me, stealing the lead. I pretend to get mad, nipping her sleek tail feathers. But, secretly, I crave her sweetgrass scent that flows over me on the wind.

Willo and Dad chatter away behind me, catching up on stories of a lost year that will be told again and again under the midnight sun.

The question now is, where, exactly?

Since I got Yellowknife out of my system, my inner navigator has been screaming for attention, yanking me along to some mysterious destination that seems to lie way above tree line. This doesn't feel anything like the raw instinct that dragged me back to the place where I hatched. Not instinct but intuition. What Dad calls a "sixth sense" that only runs in a few Plebeian families.

Like ours, I guess.

Another thing that keeps nagging me, big time, is that dream. It's waiting for me every time I fall asleep—the glowing flyway, the hole in the clouds, the silvery birds, the giant raven standing in a Tundra lake.

I get a strong hunch there must be a connection.

Another few thousand wingbeats north and there's not a tree in sight.

I watch the Tundra rolling slowly beneath us like some big mossy sea. Wet snow still covers parts of it, but most of the ponds are thawed, the source of endless bugs that we've been feasting on. It's early June. The air is pleasantly warm and ringing with the songs of many birds I've never heard before.

This seems way too easy. We've crossed the forbidden

frontier from the Boreal to the Tundra and life's never tasted sweeter.

Then I remember a line from Dad's star story about the giant raven ... *So terrifying no bird could live within a hundred million wingbeats of it and hope to survive ...* That one line, plus Dad's promise that, *Stars can't lie*, begin to strangle the thrill of finally making it to the Tundra.

If there's something sinister waiting for us out here, we must be getting awfully close.

I've resisted talking to Dad about anything related to stars. With none in the sky, why bother? Why risk leaking my secret to him?

He still doesn't know.

But with this creepy feeling that something's lurking just over the horizon, I finally get the guts to ask him.

I slip back to him with Peevo at my side. "So, Dad," I say, diving right in, "what about this giant raven story, anyway? I mean, is that really what's kept nighthawks off the Tundra forever?"

"Why do you ask?"

"I don't know. I've been thinking a lot about it."

He shoots me a probing look. "And *dreaming* about it?"

I shrug. "Maybe, now and then."

"Lots?"

"I guess so. So what does it mean?"

Dad looks up at the sky as if reading the invisible stars.

I saw that look so many times when we were chicks.

"There are a lot of stories up there, Wisp. If you're lucky, if you pay attention, one of them may call you. The only way a story gains meaning is if some nighthawk answers that call. That's how our stories grow."

"How do I do that?"

"I don't know, Wisp. That story has called you here. So I guess ... only you can answer it."

"You mean the giant raven could be *real*?" Willo asks.

"It sounds like it's up to your brother to find out," Dad says. "I'm no expert. I've never been this far north."

I feel a jolt like I've just flown into a brick wall. "But I thought you—"

"Oh, I've been to the tree line a couple of times. Watched the rivers of caribou fanning north. But the Tundra has never called me like it's called you. I'm as curious as you are about the giant raven. But what interests me even more is why *you* have been called here."

"Somehow," Peevo says, "I don't think it's to hide out here all alone, doing cool flight stunts and stuffing yourself with mosquitoes."

Everyone gets a good chuckle out of that. Even the ravens, who, I realize, have crowded behind us and been listening with keen interest.

"We will protect you from thees nasty raven," Gonzo says. "As long as you find us some careeboo, tasty bird!"

Lots of approving "*Keer-uck! Keer-uck!*" calls from his new friends.

I feel safer already.

But it turns out this is a promise Gonzo can't keep. We lose all his buddies at the first sighting of a caribou. I spot a big herd of them, mostly mothers and calves, running in the opposite direction. All the ravens spin around at once and go chasing after them, hoping for a wolf to take one out. All but Gonzo who, as tickled as he is to finally see caribou, sticks with us.

"There are lots more where those came from, no?" he says.

"Lots, Gonzo," Dad says.

Gonzo must've known from the look in my eye that I wasn't about to stop, and I think he still sees himself as my protector. Not a bad arrangement when stalking a giant raven—or being stalked by it.

Soon after we pass the caribou, I feel like I'm flying straight into my dream.

Sometime around midnight, when the Arctic sun makes a passing nod toward the horizon, a thin veil of clouds rolls in from the north. As it swallows the sun, the air suddenly chills and we rise above the cloud to get back into sunshine and grab what warmth we can. All the while, I have been tweaking my flight path, following the increasingly precise cues and commands of my inner navigator.

More reliable than even the stars.

Then, that eerie feeling again, as my flyway starts to bend downward, pulling me closer and closer to the cloud and to whatever lies below it.

Peevo, Dad, Willo, and Gonzo follow my every move. Without saying anything, they've agreed to leave all course adjustments entirely to me.

It hits me that not even Dad has been this far north.

Maybe no nighthawk. Ever.

Maybe this is what it feels like to be a Navigator.

The mysterious force seems to gain power as I descend. Just like my dream, there's that same sense of welcoming, of totally belonging here. Just like my dream, I'm tempted to simply fold my wings and let this force pull me along to its source.

But this is no dream. This is real. And I'm slowly but surely starting to panic over what lies below the cloud.

My flyway begins to break up, then disintegrate completely. I close my eyes and try to focus. Nothing comes.

I feel lost in a way I never have before.

I turn to my teacher for help. "Dad ... I can't ..."

"Just concentrate, Wisp. Focus. Fear's your biggest enemy. Don't let it block you."

I close my eyes again. Darkness. Turbulence. Chaos. *"Dad!"*

"Don't let it block you!"

The more I fight my fear, the stronger it seems to get. My wings start shaking like all my feathers will fly off.

"Wisp," Peevo cries. "Hang on. You can do this."

Do I trust her but not myself?

Peevo's voice gives me strength, not to fight but to focus.

My wings stop trembling. The darkness lifts from behind my eyes. I get it back. The force comes back.

I know where to go.

I shoot through a gauzy hole in the cloud and behold the biggest, blackest raven that ever was.

35

FINDING HOME
Raven Island

"That was a nifty piece of navigating," Peevo says, "to home in on this particular island all the way from Ecuador."

I shrug. "Heck, lots of birds cross the planet and can pinpoint a teeny nest on a particular branch on a particular tree in a particular forest in a—"

Peevo plants a wing on my beak. "*Stop!* I get your point. But don't you see the difference?"

"Not exactly," I say, drinking in her scent.

"They've been there before. They're returning to a familiar place. Just closing the loop. You didn't even know where you were going."

I flick her wing off my face. "Well, thanks for that."

Peevo laughs. "No, I mean, you didn't even know what

your target was. That your journey would end at this amazing place."

I look out from our rocky perch to the sparkling water and dazzling ice pans of a perfectly round Tundra lake. The sky is alive with hundreds of clacking Arctic terns, wheeling above our heads, protecting their nests from aerial predators. Gonzo has already befriended the terns—having promised not to eat their young. He's even convinced them to show him their favorite fishing spots.

Never trust a raven?

Dad and Willo are out hunting for botflies and warble flies, black flies and crane flies, and, no doubt, mosquitoes. The bugs here are *incredible*.

I brush a wing across the glistening bedrock. "In all my travels, I've never seen a rock this black."

"That's because it probably fell out of the sky."

"Right."

"No, really."

"This huge island is shaped exactly like a raven and you're telling me it flew in from outer space?"

"Might've. Look at the shape of this lake. As round as a blueberry. Could be an impact crater."

"Where do you learn all this stuff?"

"You've seen shooting stars?"

"Well, yeah."

"Think shooting star, only bigger."

"This island was once a big shooting star?"

"That's one way of looking at it. I mean, really big."

Once there was a giant raven that lived alone on the Tundra. It was so big it blotted out the stars when it flew...

I look up at the brilliant Arctic sky, realizing I have no idea whether it's night or day. It could be midnight, for all I know. Maybe someday I'll learn how to read the stars that hide behind all this light. For now, I don't need them. I've found something better. Something no clouds or storms or fear can take from me.

I feel a shift inside, like something big is dropping into place.

Like this island.

I have to rest my beak on its impossibly black rock. The giant raven. The silvery birds tucked in its feathers. The Tundra lake. Even a star.

It all fits.

Nothing scary here.

I start thinking about what this discovery might really mean. For me, for my family, for my Colony. I lift my head and look hard at Peevo. "You gave me some kind of to-do list back on the prairie. Something about a *special project*. What was all that about again?"

"One. Get Flare out of your life."

"Check."

"Two. Prove that nighthawks can live out here."

"Looks pretty good to me. Check."

"Three. Spread the good news to the rest of the Colony."

"Plebes, you mean."

Peevo teasingly flashes her gilded wingbars at me. "With the odd exception."

"I'll say odd."

"I don't know any Guardians or Royals who could ever *find* this place, let alone take it from us."

"Great, but how do we tell others about it?"

I hear the familiar flaps of Dad and Willo. "I can tell them," Dad says as he flutters down beside us.

"What?" I say.

"Before you even made it to Yellowknife, I was planning to fly south and meet the Colony on its way back to the Boreal."

"You'd go alone?"

Willo laughs. "Is that so strange for this family?"

"I know your mother would love this place. Others will follow."

"See?" Peevo says.

"Other vagrants like us," I say.

"Correction," Peevo says. "You're not a vagrant, Wisp. You're not a random leaf in the wind. You are a *vanguard*, remember? A leader. From the Amazon to the Arctic."

Willo lifts a wing and runs her beak through her buffy breast feathers. "Hey, I could use some company, too, you know."

Dad chuckles. "Who knows?" he says. "This might be the start of a whole new colony."

I think of the Refugium and how I might have spent my last days in the Hutch if Gonzo and Peevo hadn't saved us. "What about a winter home?"

"We could look for a new one. There's still lots of rainforest out there."

I lay a wing across Peevo's long, tapered back. "Special project, eh?"

"Time for a new story, Wisp."

The story my mind keeps drifting back to, the one that helped save all our skins, was about the fish-eating ravens.

"So, like, that stuff about the white-feathered raven clan. Did Gonzo and those beach bums really descend from bald eagles?"

Peevo tucks in beside me. "Nah, I made all that up. Thought it would make them feel important."

"What about the fish-eating bit?"

"Made that up, too."

"But ... Gonzo's so *good* at it."

"Good teacher, I guess. I thought it might stop him from eating you. At least, for a day or two."

Something pops in the center of my chest. It triggers a giant belly laugh that launches me into the Arctic sky. I climb ten thousand wingbeats above the sun-washed Tundra.

My wings twitch. My muscles tense. I lift my head.

Beerb ... Beerb ... Beerb.

At the dawn of a new day and a new life, I gaze down at the giant raven that called me here. The sight of it knocks me out of the sky.

I fall into a dead-drop dive. My screaming feathers send shivers of delight from beak to tail.

V-R-R-R-O-O-O-O-O-M!

I claim the Tundra as a home.

And it claims me.

Acknowledgements

My heartfelt thanks to ...

Birdman extraordinaire, Joachim Obst, for sharing your thrilling story of a lone nighthawk soaring where it shouldn't—over the tundra at Daring Lake, Northwest Territories. I tell everybody, "That's my Wisp!"

Bird guru, Arthur Cleveland Bent, for your intimate study of nighthawks nesting on a pebbled school roof.

Ecologist, Suzanne Carrière, for your thoughts about the small percentage of nighthawks that are "adventurous."

PhD student, Erin Baerwald, for helping me find the best scientific research on nighthawks (and confirming the color of their poop).

Jack Panayi, for giving me advice on the story as only a twelve-year-old can—and for naming Gonzo!

My daughter Nimisha, and her *amiga* Ana Leticia De Leon,

for helping my birds and animals talk intelligible Spanish. *¡Muchisimas gracias!*

My wife Brenda, for your fine-tooth combing of the manuscript and unflagging support of my writing habit.

Peter Carver for, as usual, finding the fire behind the smoke of my early drafts and helping me build a sturdy bridge into the world of talking animals.

Sharon Fitzhenry, Richard Dionne, and all the skilled crew at Red Deer Press and Fitzhenry & Whiteside for supporting this book from start to finish.

And to the Canada Council for the Arts whose generous support made this book possible.

Interview with Jamie Bastedo

What led you to write a story with a bird as your main narrator? How difficult was it to imagine what it's like to be that bird?

In my other novels, I write through the eyes of a grizzly bear, polar bear, kangaroo, thorny lizard, and lots of other animals. We can never know exactly how other creatures experience their world. But the magic of fiction is that it can bring us closer to them than any other art form. I always wanted to write a high-flying story with a bird's-eye view. The challenge was to strike a believable balance between reality and imagination, between Wisp's outer and inner worlds. To do this, I had to make sure the bird biologist and story-spinner in me were both happy.

The migratory route taken by nighthawks is quite remarkable. What was involved in doing the research so that the details of Wisp's flight would always be authentic? How many of his ports of call are you personally familiar with?

The common nighthawk has one of the longest migration distances of any bird species in North America. They often migrate in spectacular flocks, numbering in the thousands. In my research, I learned that their exact routes vary from flock to flock and from year to year, so this gave me a wide playing field when charting Wisp's incredible journey.

I make a point to "write what I know" and have personally migrated through most of the amazing landmarks along his route. The day I stood before a "walking tree" in the Ecuador rainforest, I knew I wanted to write a book set in the Amazon. I felt the same way while rambling the beaches of Central America, exploring Arizona's mysterious Canyon de Chelly, and doing a movie shoot in the bubbling landscape of Wyoming's Yellowstone National Park. I got hooked on volcanoes in Hawaii—almost fell into one!—and so was happy to find Popocatépetl under a Mexican flyway. Big cities are a major challenge for migrating birds, especially at night, so I chose the one I know best, Calgary. I have watched great flocks of migrating nighthawks while driving a grain truck on the prairies. As for the Boreal Forest, that's where I live; it's the land I love most. And the Tundra has been a place of work and play for me ever since I migrated north many years ago. Have I personally seen a nighthawk out there? Not yet—but stay tuned!

Your story shows how nighthawks rely on a variety of navigational cues to guide their migratory journey, from stars and landmarks to the mysterious force sensed by Wisp's "inner navigator." How much do we really know about what birds are steering by when they migrate?

"How do birds migrate?" is one of the greatest unsolved scientific questions around. Stellar navigation is believed to be among the most important navigational cues and that's why I give it special importance in the story. Other possible cues include the Earth's magnetic field, prevailing winds, major landmarks, and movements of the sun. I discovered a paper that describes the nighthawk's "hypothetical sense of location or orientation" that launched me into the magical world of Wisp's inner navigator—"more reliable than even the stars!"

You enjoy telling stories that are rooted in the natural environment. What is it about this species—nighthawks—that made Wisp's story an important one to tell?

Because of the nighthawk's piercing calls, its weird booming dive, and the crazy way it flies, this species grabs the attention of people who may have no special interest in birds. I find that anyone who spends any time in the outdoors usually has some kind of nighthawk story to tell—from hearing spooky noises at night, to having one silently whoosh past the tip of their nose. Yet this species is one of the most mysterious and misunderstood birds in North America. Often mistaken for hawks or falcons, nighthawks once had a bounty on their heads and were shot by the

thousands. What's worrisome today is that their numbers—
like many other long-range migrants—are nose-diving. So
I chose this bird for two reasons: it's really cool, and it's
threatened. I wanted more people to know and care about
this amazing bird.

**There are certain species in the animal kingdom that
do have a kind of class system—wolves, for example. Is
there any evidence to suggest that this kind of hierarchy
also can be found among species of birds—thinking of
the Plebes and Guardians in this story?**

Just like bears, dogs, or zebras, nighthawks are not robots.
Each one is different. Laboratory studies of bird behavior
show that some individuals may be more aggressive, more
adventurous, or faster to learn. But I don't have to look to
science to prove this. All I need to do is go out to my backyard
chicken coop and watch my hens for five minutes. Bullies
and victims are well defined in my little chicken society
of a dozen birds. In my make-believe nighthawk society,
Plebeians are at the bottom of the pecking order. But Wisp
does not take the blows lying down.

**For various reasons, some species have changed their
migratory routes in recent years and can be found in
areas of the world where they once did not travel to
or dwell in. What are the most important reasons for
this change?**

Over almost thirty years, I have witnessed several new
species push north into the woods near my Yellowknife

home—for example, cougars, coyotes, white-tailed deer, and black-billed magpies. Somebody was the first. Somebody led his or her species into a completely foreign territory. What got them moving? Science has no answers, only guesses. Climate change, famine, storms, navigation problems, rivalry with others, youthful inexperience, or simple wanderlust may all play a part. Or it may be some eerie planetary force we've never thought of. As a fiction writer, I love to play with such scientific mysteries.

A lot of the comic relief in this story is provided by Gonzo the raven. Why does the raven lend itself to this kind of portrayal?

For those who don't live around ravens, it may be hard to believe that they really do fly upside down, can outwit deadly predators like coyotes and wolves, and have a virtually limitless vocabulary of trills, squawks, and croaks. Yellowknife has one of the highest raven densities anywhere and I regularly watch them at play right outside my kitchen window. Ravens, and their cousins, the crows, jays, and magpies, are believed to be the smartest birds on Earth. Native stories around the world give them magical powers with a hearty dose of humor—just like my Gonzo.

Sometimes different species find it useful to inhabit the same territory and exist peacefully side by side—for example, flocks of pelicans and cormorants often can be seen flying together and fishing out of the same lakes in some parts of Canada. Is there any evidence to suggest

that nighthawks and ravens could co-exist in the same way—or is the connection between Wisp, Willo, and Gonzo totally fictional? Are there other bird species that co-exist easily?

Charles Darwin, the father of evolution, drew much inspiration from watching how different finch species on the Galapagos Islands could live almost on top of each other as long as they ate different foods. Gonzo loves fresh meat (and the odd soggy doughnut). Wisp loves bugs. So, no conflict there. Trouble is, Gonzo also has a taste for nighthawks. Instant conflict. But, again, every bird is different and neither Gonzo nor Wisp could be considered "normal." As they journey north, their unlikely friendship feeds on their growing need for each other. In this sense, Wisp boldly crosses forbidden borders not only between territories but also between species.

Wisp is called a "vagrant" by some of his fellow nighthawks. In human experience, a vagrant is one who has no visible home or means of support; it's a term of disapproval. Is it the same for birds like Wisp?

Early in the story, Arwen brands Wisp as a vagrant, spitting out the word "like she'd swallowed acid." Flare refers to Wisp as a "slippery vagrant" and later, full of contempt, calls his father a "vagrant-breeder." In the meantime, Wisp is not sure what he is. It takes Peevo to help him see his true calling, not as a vagrant—a solo, homeless "plaything of the wind"—but a *vanguard*, a leader, who "chooses his own flyways and leads other nighthawks to a new and better life."

Wisp's journey then moves him from vagrant to vanguard, "from me to we."

What advice would you give young writers who wish to develop their own fictional stories about the natural world? What are the pitfalls they need to avoid?

Feature animals that you know well or that arouse strong feelings in you, such as affection, fear, wonder, or revulsion. Create animal characters that are unique; it's too easy to think of the "wise owl" or the "clever fox" or "raging bear." Learn all you can about your chosen animals and the places where they live. Then let your imagination loose. Think about what role humans will play in your nature story, if any. Decide whether your animals will talk, or not (either way is fun). Last, when you write your story, don't try to please anyone but yourself. If you like it—if it makes you laugh or cry or say "Wow!"—then you've got a good story. Period.

Thank you, Jamie.

Other books by Jamie Bastedo

- *On Thin Ice*
- *Sila's Revenge*
- *Free as the Wind: Saving the Horses of Sable Island*
- *Falling for Snow: A Naturalist's Journey into the World of Winter*
- *Tracking Triple Seven*
- *Shield Country: The Life and Times of the Oldest Piece of the Planet*
- *Reaching North: A Celebration of the Subarctic*
- *The Horrors: Terrifying Tales, Book Two (edited by Peter Carver)*
- *Trans Canada Trail Official Guide: Northwest Territories*